MacCormac Warriors Trilogy
Book Two

LuAnn Nies

FALLEN ANGEL

ISBN: 979-8-88653-450-4

Published by Satin Romance
An Imprint of Melange Books, LLC
White Bear Lake, MN 55110
www.satinromance.com

Published in the United States of America.

Cover Design by Caroline Andrus

Scottish and English Historical Romances have always been my favorite genres to read. Fallen Angel is the second book in the MacCormac Warriors Trilogy, and Freyja is unlike any character I have ever written.

I enjoyed watching her grow from a wounded soul into a courageous leader. I think she just might be my alter-ego.

I would like to thank my critique partners, Jill Dalton, Elyse Lawrey, and Carol Michtics for their brilliant edits and suggestions.

A special thanks to Jeff Peer for his helpful fatherly advice, and to my go-to-guy, my son Matt, who always takes the time to answer my crazy questions.

Scotland
A charming country filled with
breathtaking views, rich
history, and romance.

In the 1690s, the Highlands
is a wild and dangerous place.
'Tis a time when women would do
anything to survive, and even more
to protect those, they loved.

Tragedy and a wounded soul
forced Freyja Weir to become a fighter.
Duty and a determination for
justice made her a great leader.

One

1692 Scottish Highlands

"I donae like this," Malcolm Haywood whispered as he trotting his horse up alongside Hugh. Malcolm's head swiveled from side to side, scanning their surroundings. Commander Hugh MacCormac ignored his cousin. Hugh also studied the heavily wooded area for the likelihood of danger. This was the perfect spot for an ambush. The moon, their sole light for the past hour, slid behind a veil of dense grey clouds, casting eerie shadows across the ground that darted behind rocks and trees like children at play.

Malcolm shifted in his saddle and murmured, "Why did ye leave the main road back there to take this old footpath?"

"I hae traveled this trail years ago," Hugh replied. "The thick canopy above should protect us from the rain." He looked up and said, "I just hope the trees aren't so thick that they block out the moonlight."

The constant rain had made it nearly impossible for Hugh to see more than one horse-length ahead of them. He estimated weighed down by the caravan of supply wagons, he and the troop of warriors were a little more than two hours away from Corell Castle, their Highland home.

Nervously, Malcolm rubbed his chin and said, "It would have been wiser to have stayed another night in Edinburgh."

Hugh nodded in total agreement, but his thoughts were wrapped around the comfort of his bedchambers in the barracks. His travels had left them all cold, tired, and hungry. He wanted to stretch out and sleep in a bed instead of spending another night curled up on the cold wet ground. He preferred his large bed along with a curvaceous woman who would keep him warm through the night, and a bottle of brandy would do wonders toward restoring his soul.

He should stop to rest the horses and give the men a chance to walk off the stiffness in their legs and backs but lined up as they were on this narrow trail left them vulnerable to attack. Thankfully, Hugh hadn't seen any indication that the trail had been used recently, though if there were tracks up ahead of them, the rain would soon wash them away. He would watch for an area where the wagons could be grouped together for protection, so they could stop and rest.

His horse Perseus slowed his steady gait. Holding his head high and his ears alert, the big bay turned his head from side to side as if perceiving noises and smells a human couldn't detect. A shiver of apprehension slithered up Hugh's back.

"What's amiss with yer horse," Malcolm whispered.

"I donae ken." Hugh's sharp gaze swept amongst the bushes wondering what could be lying in wait. Riding in the Highlands at night with loaded supply wagons and only a small troop of armed men, made their group a perfect target for attacks from the many clans who constantly raided each other. Being so near to where the recent massacre of Maclain and the Glencoe MacDonalds, which had occurred only two months earlier, made Hugh uneasy. The only place safe was behind the walls of Corell Castle.

Hugh's horse's ears flicked out to the side, listening intently. He stepped gingerly, the layers of thick damp leaves covering the ground muffled the sound of his large hooves. The hair on the back of Hugh's neck and arms drew to attention.

Hugh placed his hand on the hilt of his sword and push the hilt downwards, causing the tip of his sword to rise up. A signal they had devised to alert the men behind them of an impending ambush.

"Aye," Malcolm reply.

Hugh didn't relish the idea of being accosted by rival clans or arrested by English dragoons and taken back to Fort William. He had been held there with Cameron once for a week and they barely escaped being hung. The rain had subsided, and streams of moonlight seeped through the trees as they moved cautiously along the trail.

Hugh's horse suddenly stepped to the side, bumping Malcolm's horse forcing it off the trail. His horse stopped and lowered his head as if noticing something on the ground. Hugh's gaze shot to the ground searching for a trap or anything that might pose a threat. Then he saw it. A small portion of a person's arm protruding out from under a pile of leaves.

"What do ye see?" Malcolm whispered, leaning forward.

Hugh dismounted, patted the horse's neck and handed his reins to his cousin. Cautiously, he scanned the area as he circled around the front of his horse.

"What is it?" Malcolm whispered.

"A partially buried body," Hugh murmured softly. Kneeling down Hugh brushed away the dirt and leaves from the remains. Inhaling sharply, he swore under his breath. It was a woman. Her clothes were ripped, one sleeve completely torn away. He brushed aside a long muddy braid, which revealed her badly beaten swollen face. He had seen men slaughtered in war, but he could never handle women, children, or animals being mistreated. Gripping her by the arm he eased her onto her back.

“Good Lord, she’s alive.” His stomach twisted and burned with rage.

“A woman?” The captain’s horse stomped his hoof. “How do ye suppose she got here?” Malcolm replied. “There isn’t a croft aboot here less than two days ride. And ye say she’s still alive?”

Removing his glove, Hugh picked off a leaf stuck to her cheek. He wondered what the poor lass could possibly have done to have deserved such a beating and then left to die alone in the woods. Given the severity of her punishment, she must have been accused of being a witch, a whore, or she had done something extremely evil.

The news of the half dead, beaten lass spread quickly from soldier to soldier. The nervous whispers of his men still mounted and anxious to vacate the area could be heard in the eerie silence. Glancing up toward his cousin Hugh said, “Dispatch some men to search the area for signs of who might have done this to the poor lass.”

Malcolm nodded, then turned and issued orders to the troops. Given her severe injuries, the girl would not last long in the cold. Hugh also knew she was too weak to survive the journey to Corell Castle.

“Hugh,” Malcolm whispered, “We best be moving on. ‘Tis late and these woods donae feel safe.”

Hugh glanced up; his cousin was quickly being engulfed in the thick fog.

“‘Tis too dark to see anything,” Malcolm said, glancing at the soldiers shaking their heads as they returned.

Hugh glanced back down at the woman and scratched his beard, then gently brushed the dirt and leaves back over her body. “Sorry lass. Ye’ll suffer less discomfort if I leave ye here. Though with the same result of death, I’m afraid.”

Hugh stood and walked away from the lass. He had witnessed death many times, and though she clung to life, he knew there wasn’t anything he could do to help her. Gathering his reins he swung up onto the big bay's back. They rode the next two hours in silence. His men were weary and cold, yet the seasoned soldiers remained alert and watchful.

~

Even though the rain had stopped and they finally rode through the gates of Corell Castle, Hugh felt miserable. Hugh dismounted, and without a word, relinquished his reins to a stable boy, then headed for the keep. He needed to work the kinks out of his sore body and put his thoughts in order.

Over the past two hours he had struggled with how to inform Cameron of the woman they had found half buried, and his choice to leave her there. He had contemplated going back and properly burying her. Could she have been one of the MacDonalds who escaped, only to be found and beaten. How was Cam going to respond to that news. The decision of what, if anything, should be done about the lass would be left up to his chief. Laird Cameron MacCormac, chieftain of the MacCormac clan, happened to be his cousin and close friend since his birth. They were schooled side by side. Cameron was groomed to take over as Laird when his father passed. Hugh had been trained to fight at Cam's side and to take over as Laird if his cousin were killed. But Hugh's life had considerably changed when Cam married Lady Adriana, and their son, little Robbie, was born. The lad would someday become Laird of the MacCormac clan in the event of his father's death.

After being promoted to commander of the MacCormac army, Hugh's position required him to leave Corell Castle and his cousin's side. He was frequently assigned to patrols and to escort supply shipments. At eight and twenty, he had thought by now he would have something to call his own and wouldn't still be living in the barracks. He recognized that something was missing in his life. Truth was, he was lonely and wanted a family of his own.

Stopping at the bottom of the stone steps which led up to the keep, Hugh wearily rubbed both hands over his face, then dug his fingers deep into his beard and scratched his jaw. Without much enthusiasm, he trudged up the steps and entered the keep.

The great hall was filled with folks having supper and avoiding the miserable weather. The warmth from the fires and tantalizing aroma of roasted meats, vegetables, and spiced breads filled the hall. Hugh spotted Cam at the high table next to his wife, Lady Adriana. He started toward his cousin but paused when he heard his name called.

"Hugh," Lady Adriana's lady's maid Bethany, called out in a loud whisper as she scurried toward him. "'Tis aboot time ye returned," she said, handing him a steaming mug. "We almost gave ye up for dead."

"Aye," he said after taking a long drink and wiping his arm across his mouth. "I thank ye, Bethany. Big Alec is a lucky mon to hae such a loving wench to greet him each night."

She giggled, then dismissed his remark. "Maddy said to saved ye some venison and turkey." She handed him a large package wrapped in waxed cloth. "Noo, ye drink down yer broth and get yerself into some dry clothes."

"I'd kiss ye lass but I donae need Big Alec hunting me down and relieving me of my head this night."

She grinned and collected his empty mug. With her free hand she patted his chest, and said, "Go on with ye noo. Ye look as if yer gonna drop where ye stand." She turned and sauntered back toward the kitchen stairs.

Hugh turned and saw Cam, and his lovely family start up the steps that led to their bedchambers. His report will have to hold until tomorrow.

Back in his own chambers in the barracks, Hugh placed his wet boots by the fire. He stripped off his wet clothes and hung them on the drying rope next to his bed. He needed a hot bath, but it was too late to rouse someone to heat and haul water. He settled into his bed, sighed, and within seconds drifted off to sleep, only to toss and turn until he awoke tangled in his blankets. The lass's battered face lingered in his mind. Who was she. Who were her people and where had she come from? Guilt of not doing more for the woman drove him from his bed. He dug out dry clothes from his trunk and donned them, then slipped back into his damp boots. He grabbed the wrapped meat and went to saddle his horse, Perseus. It didn't take him long to ready the big bay, and soon he was heading back to where the girl was buried.

Without supply wagons slowing him down, Hugh soon reached the edge of the woods. The rain had stopped, and the sky cleared. Moonlight illuminated the trail, allowing Hugh to find the shallow grave. However, in his haste, he had forgotten to grab a shovel from the gardener's shed. Swearing under his breath, he dismounted and tied his horse to a tree. He kicked the leaves and ground cover aside until he found a branch thick enough with which to dig. He knelt down next to the woman and brushed the leaves and dirt from her face. His plan was to pull the woman's body from the shallow grave, drag her further into the woods and bury her in a proper grave. It did not matter to him what she might have done to get to this place, he'd been raised a Christian, and it was his duty to see the lass received a proper Christian burial.

Hugh pulled her long braid from the dirt and placed it across her chest. He made the sign of the cross then bent down and reached under her arms and pulled. A loud grunt slid between his lips. The body didn't budge. *This is no wee lass.* With more determination, he squatted down, hooked his arms under hers, then clasped his hands together under her breast. Inhaling a long breath, Hugh pulled with all his strength. The body dislodged from the shallow grave causing him to fall back. He ended up sitting on the ground with his legs spread wide and the woman's body sprawled across his lap. Growling, he pushed her to the side and tried to crawl out from under her. Then he heard a soft moan. Hugh froze. "Jesus, Mary, and Joseph. I never thought to check if ye were still alive. Noo, what am I to do with ye?"

This new development definitely altered his plans. Foremost, if she were possibly a survivor of the MacDonald clan, just being here could have severe ramifications for him and his own clan.

Until he learned who she was, he needed to keep her hidden and away from Corell Castle. Unfortunately, this lass would not make it through the night if exposed to the elements in her condition. It was dangerous, but being the God-fearing man he was, he needed to find a warm, dry place in which to take her, if he was to try and save her life.

After weighing his options, the ancient hunting lodge on Loch Morar where he and Cam used to hunt and fish, came to mind. As far as Hugh knew the stone building had been closed up after the old laird's death. Although it had not been kept up, he could start a fire, and the place would at least keep the rain off them for the night.

Scrambling to his feet Hugh glanced around checking to see if anyone might have returned to make sure the woman was dead. He pulled her up as if he expected her to stand, and she wabbled like his cousin Malcolm once he'd passed out from too much drink. With a great grunt, he shoved her body up against his horse's side. After adjusting his grip, he pushed her up and onto the horse's neck. Once she was positioned and he felt she wouldn't fall, he swung his leg up over the horse behind her. Hugh pulled her across his lap hoping to make her more comfortable. He glanced around again, praying no one witnessed him robbing a grave, and nudged his horse forward.

The woman's dead weight was heavy and hard to hang on to. Once again, the pale light from the moon disappeared behind thick black clouds and after a spell, it began to rain again. They finally reached the eastern shore of Lock Morar and followed the trail south. Perseus picked his way along the rocky, forgotten trail that lead to the old MacCormac hunting lodge.

It had taken Hugh much longer than he thought to reach the lodge. He was cold, wet, sore from riding most of the day, and exhausted as he reined his horse in by the lodge door. He pushed the woman from his lap back onto his horse's neck and dismounted. He anticipated the needle-like-pain that radiate through his numb feet and legs as he stepped down from his horse and touched the ground.

After a moment he pulled the woman from his horse with a loud groan. "Och, woman. Yer five and ten stones if yer one."

He struggled to get her repositioned in his arms, then stumbled to the lodge and kicked the door open. The room was shrouded in dark shadows. He hoped he remembered where everything was and crossed to where a narrow bed once set against the wall. When he bumped into the side of it with his leg, he leaned over and set the woman down. Straightening, he stretched and rubbed his back, then crossed to the hearth. He filled the hearth with what little scraps of wood there was left in a basket and built a fire. The low flames offered little light to the gloomy space, although enough for him to see the woman's breasts rise as she drew air into her lungs. He returned outside and led his horse into a covered, two-sided shed in the fenced in paddock. He unsaddled the horse and carried his sodden leather gear and blanket into the lodge.

Wet and half froze, Hugh removed his boots and placed them by the fire, then stripped off his clothes and hung them over the chairs to dry.

Naked and shivering, he turned to the woman sprawled across the bed. Her clothes were filthy, wet, and half torn from her body. If her wounds didn't kill her, she would surely freeze to death in what was left of her clothes. It may not be proper to undress her, but nothing about the situation was proper, and he could not let her stay as she was.

Hugh made quick work of untying her petticoats and

tossing them aside. His large half frozen fingers fumbled with the laces on her ankle boots, but once removed, he pulled down her stockings and dropped them on the floor. Sitting her upright, he removed her torn bodice and shift and was pleased to find she wore no corset for him to remove. Since he could not see her clearly, he brushed his hands over her body searching for open wounds with protruding bones. Not finding any wounds other than lumps and abrasions, which he could tend to in the morning light, he grabbed a thin wool blanket and covered her. Gathering up what was left of her clothes, he quickly laid them by the fire, then carefully crawled under the blanket behind her and pulled her cold body back against his. Normally, he would have appreciated the fullness of her curves and the predicament he found himself. Except, at the moment he prayed the warmth of his body would keep her alive throughout the night. He had no desire to awake snuggled up against a lass who had died during the night.

In the morning, if she lived, he would question her. He would find out who she was, and who had left her in the woods to die.

Two

Freyja longed to stay wrapped in the warmth and protection that engulfed her. A deep groan emanated from behind her, followed by a lengthy sigh. Warm breath tickled her neck and sent a delightful shiver down her spine. She did not wish to awaken from the security and contentment of her dream, so she relaxed and soaked in the warmth. Little by little she inched her way back to reality. She blinked several times as she took in her surroundings. Nothing about the small room looked familiar.

Something heavy lay over her side, then she detected the steady breathing of someone behind her. Her chest tightened, she struggled to control the fear quickly growing inside of her. Holding her breath she listened, forcing her brain to recall who it might be and how she came to be inside the small stone structure.

An enormous hand, which laid across her abdomen, pulled her body backwards until it molded perfectly to the soft hair tickling her backside.

Freyja came fully awake and realized she was naked and lying in front of a man who she feared was also naked. She didn't dare move. What would he do if she woke him? A large, calloused hand leisurely slid up and cupped her breast. The man sighed and snuggled in closer. He moaned softly into her hair as something long and hard pressed against her buttocks.

A wave of panic surged over Freyja, and she leaped off the bed. Foggy and lightheaded, she tried to control her balance so not to fall. Her body shook from a sudden onslaught of pain and adrenalin, and a strange sensation she could not name.

The man sat up.

His long auburn hair hung wildly over his tanned chest and wide shoulders giving him the appearance of a beautiful, wild creature. Her heart slammed against her ribs.

The man grabbed a fistful of blanket and yanked it up to cover himself. His piercing amber eyes slowly swept over her nakedness.

Although Freyja felt hot and flushed from standing before him naked, she refused to let that fact appear as if it affected her. Clenching her fist, she tried to slow her breathing and forced her body to stand tall. The tiny hairs on the back of her neck rose, and her head pounded as if a stampede of horses raced through it. Yet, she was determined to show this man, whomever he was, that she was calm and in control and would not be taken down as easily as he might think.

She raised her chin and glared down her noise at him. Oh, she recognized the repulsed expression on his face. Most men did not approve of her tall, muscular frame, or the rigorous training routine she put herself through each day. While her reward had always been witnessing their defeat at her hands in the training ring, she did not need this man's or any other man's approval. Never again.

Freyja's head felt heavy, and she struggled to hold it upright. She licked her dry lips and said, "What do you think you are doing? Did you believe you would actually get away with this? You should be ashamed of yerself."

His eyes rounded at her statement, and he moved as if to rise up off the bed. With an unsteady hand she brushed a clump of matted hair to one side of her face. Noticing an iron fire poker leaning against the heath, Freyja spun around and grabbed it then turned back to face him. Her hands shook as she held the iron rod out like a sword. She raked her teeth over her lower lip and demanded, "Who are you? Where am I, and how did I get here?"

The huge man's nostrils flared as he inhaled deeply, his chest expanded then relaxed as he exhaled slowly. With a bearlike paw he reached up and stroked a hand down over his thick reddish-brown mustache and beard. His gaze held hers with intense scrutiny, as if he strived to see inside her head and read her thoughts.

Without any warning, a crippling pain seized Freyja. She closed her eyes and swayed, dropping the poker as she stumbled back a couple of steps.

Damn, I'm going to faint.

Powerful arms swept her up and gently placed her back on the bed. The man drew the blankets up and over her. They were still warm from where they both had slept only moments before. Freyja opened her eyes and found the man had donned his trews. "What happened to me?" she whispered, rubbing her temples to ease the pain. Her voice sounded as weak as she suddenly felt.

"I am anxious to hear yer tale myself, lass. Do ye remember how ye came to be in the woods?"

He had a strong, deep, commanding voice, one Freyja felt certain instructed men, like an army. Her eyes widened. Were there soldiers camped outside? Had they returned and found she had not died? She needed to see who they were. She struggled to sit up.

"Easy lass, yer hurt verra bad." Two large hands gently pressed her shoulders back to the pillow. "Yer gonna hae to stay abed a few days." His expression had turned from disgusted to pity. Freyja turned her face away from him. She disliked being pitied or treated like a defenseless woman.

She had trained alongside her brothers and the other soldiers to prove she could handle herself. Her eyes filled with tears. The only thing she actually proved was that she wasn't strong enough to protect anyone when tested.

I'm so sorry, Andrew. I let you down, and I will never see you again.

"Lass, donae cry. Tell me what happened to ye. Mayhap I can help ye." He paused, and when she did not reply or turn to look at him, added, "At least I can return ye to yer family where ye'll be safe and looked after."

Panic boiled anew. How was she to feel safe if he returned her to her family? She would never be safe again. She could never return to her home. Home, the word alone squeezed her heart. She no longer had a home nor a family.

"Lass, ye rest. I am gonna fetch ye some water."

He slipped his shirt over his head and stepped into his tall boots. As he grabbed his leather jack and sword belt he glanced back at her. The deep tanned lines on his ruggedly handsome face softened.

"Yer safe here. Ye've nothing to fear, least of all from me." He pulled the door open, ducked through the opening then pulled it shut behind him.

Safe from him? What a great warrior she was. She hadn't even seen his sword lying there. She could have been free now; except where could she go? Freyja fidgeted with the frayed edge of the old worn blanket. Wouldn't Finlay laugh at her predicament. Was that it? Was this man one of Finlay's men? Had he been sent to find her body, to make sure she was truly dead, or had he been sent to finish her off? She glanced toward the door.

Spying her ripped clothes draped over the chairs in front of the hearth, she drug the blanket from the bed and wrapped it around her shoulders and scrambled to her feet. She prayed he would be gone long enough for her to search the stone cottage for weapons. The dizziness was gone for now, but the pounding in her head had returned. She made her way to the door and slid the bolt over, locking it. As she slipped on the now dry dress she wore helping with chores around the castle, she noticed the many bruises and scrapes that covered her body.

If this man had been sent to finish the task, he would have to do better than Torcall and Dunn. Freyja paused, if he had wanted to kill her, why had he gone to such lengths to save her?

He doesn't know who I am. But what does he want with me?

Freyja cast a quick glance around. The room appeared much larger with the morning light streaming in through the two smeared windows. There appeared to be a couple additional rooms in the back part of the structure, and she noted to investigate them later.

A knock sounded at the door. Freyja grabbed the fire poker and turned toward the door. "Lass, may I enter?"

She paused. *He hadn't tried the handle.* "One moment." She crossed to the door, slid the bolt back and opened the thick wooden door.

He entered, and she watched him closely. In one arm he carried an armful of firewood, in the other a bucket of water. He crossed the room and placed the bucket and firewood by the hearth. His shirt stretched tight across his wide back and shoulders. His legs where thick and muscular. When he turned, his bushy brows pulled together as he took in her appearance and glanced at the poker she once again pointed at his chest. He towered over her height of five foot ten by almost a half-foot and Freyja had to tilt her head all the way back to keep eye contact with him.

"Who are you?" she demanded, glancing around the room. "And where am I?"

His voice was low and deep, and gentle when he answered, "My name is Hugh MacCormac. I am cousin and commander for the MacCormac chief. Yer in the MacCormac's old hunting lodge on Loch Morar. We are aboot nineteen kilometers from Corell Castle."

"What are your plans for me," she asked, willing her body not to tremble. She didn't like being vulnerable and defenseless. The man was huge and could take her head off with the swipe of one hand if he pleased. Though it had never been an easy task for her in the past, she would do well to keep a tight rein on her temper and sharp tongue. His mesmerizing, amber eyes studied her closely. When he spoke, the tone of his deep voice sent warm quivers through her body.

"I donae know what to do with ye till I be known who ye are and what happened to ye." He fisted his hands and placed them on his narrow hips.

She had no desire to divulge her name to a commander for the MacCormac. If she did, he would cart her off to her home where she certainly would hang. Though the poker did not weigh much more than a stable cat, her battered arm ached from pointing the iron rod at him.

"Set yer weapon down. Let us sit and discuss yer situation." He gestured toward the chairs by the table. He crossed to the table, pulled one chair aside and settled his bulky frame onto it. His back slightly turned to her.

Her *situation?* Freyja contemplated hitting him over the head with the poker but as weak as she felt right then she didn't think the big dumb *numpty* would even feel it. The loss of her home, her beloved brother Andrew, and her own life was more serious than a mere *situation*.

Freyja returned the poker to the hearth, and with more force than needed she jerked a chair over to the table and plopped down upon it. She felt her lips purse as she tried to control her emotions. It would be no service to her to lose her temper now. She needed to try and gain control of this *situation*.

"Weel, lass. Are ye gonna be telling me who ye are? I am expected elsewhere, and I would be knowing yer name afore I go." He squinted as he examined her, waiting for her to reveal all her secrets to him. His face was bronzed and creased with deep lines at the outer edges of his eyes, and around his mouth from years spent riding, training, and fighting in the sun. She wondered at his age. He wasn't old enough to be her father, but certainly old enough to be an uncle or older brother. Far older than her age of ten and nine.

"Weel, lass. Hae ye suddenly lost yer tongue?"

Freyja cleared her throat and blinked a few times. "I cannot recall my name." She rubbed her temples and added, "And I do not remember what happen to me before I awoke this morning."

His piercing eyes narrowed as he studied her, considering if she spoke the truth or not. He didn't seem to believe her tale. Well, she didn't care what he believed or thought about her. She was not used to answering to anyone other than Andrew.

After a long moment he finally spoke. "As ye wish. Just know yer safe here. No one will bother ye." He shoved a package wrapped in waxed cloth across the table toward her. "There's plenty of meat in here." His gaze raked over her, and he added, "I will bring ye something more suitable to wear when I return this evening."

She didn't reply, though she wished she knew what he was thinking. He shook his head as if he were frustrated then stood and walked to the door. Only to stop and turn back to stare at her for a moment longer. "Anything ye be wanting me to bring ye?" She shook her head. She didn't need anything from him or any other man.

The huge warrior paused for a moment longer then walked out.

Freyja quickly unwrapped the meat and found a large hunk of roast venison and a thick slab of turkey. She took a bit of the moist turkey, closed her eyes she savored the wonderful flavor. Her teeth and the right side of her face ached with each bite, but she was too hungry to care. She knew as filthy as she was, that she must look dreadful. If her face was bruised as badly as it felt, she must be a terrible sight.

His repulsed expression at seeing her naked was one she had seen before. Her body looked different from the other girls at Dreki Craige Castle. She grew until she'd become as tall as her brothers. Her hips and shoulders were wide, and her breast were too large in proportion to her narrow waist. When her brothers and the other children started to tease her, it wasn't long before she'd enquired on how to use a sword and a dirk. Soon she had numerous soldiers offering to instruct her.

Her thoughts turned to her family. They had once been a loving family, but once her parents were both gone everything changed. Freyja closed her eyes when tears threatened and pushed them away. She refused to let herself cry over all that she had lost. There were too many things which required her full attention right now. She was counting on her years of training to help her through this *situation*, as the big warrior with the amazing amber eyes referred to her life as.

Exhaling a long breath, Freyja assured herself that her only options were to survive, heal, and regain her strength. Not sure how or when, but she would return to Dreki Craige Castle, and Finlay, Torcall, and Gunn would pay for what they had done--at the end of her sword.

~

Hugh tossed his saddle up onto Perseus's back, secured the leather straps, and mounted. It didn't feel right leaving the lass alone, but the hunting lodge would be hard to see tucked back in amongst the trees. The woman should be safe. Though, if she truly could not remember her name and what had happened to her, she may be still in danger from whomever attacked her. He would have to hurry. He kicked his horse into a gallop.

The infuriating woman held a tight grip on Hugh's thoughts as he made his way back to Corell Castle. He'd saved her life, yet she anticipated he planned to hurt her. She should have been grateful to him for coming back and removing her from her grave and giving her the warmth of his body throughout the night. Instead, he had been jolted from a sound sleep when she jumped from the bed and confronted him like a crazed warrior. Not ashamed of her nakedness, but strong, proud and determined to fight him. He wondered who had trained her to fight. Her shapely body displayed bruises and scrapes, and many old scars. Her thick hair was caked in mud and plastered to her head. Her tanned skin and greenish-blue, almond shaped eyes gave her a striking appearance. Cleaned up and eliminate her bruises, she would be a bonnie lass.

With the well-defined muscles in her arms and legs, and what appeared to be dried blood and skin beneath her jagged nails, she had put up a good fight against her attacker. Which most likely had saved her life. Yet, he feared her severe bruises were caused by more than one mere man. What horrible act had she done to warrant such treatment? Maybe she learned someone's secrets. Secrets she was supposed to take with her to the grave.

When she had fainted, he had caught her in his arms, he'd been stunned that he hadn't wished to put her down. He had a strong urge to hold and protect her, but until he knew who she was and what really had happened to her, he couldn't do much to help her. Hugh's stomach twisted when he realized that she could be married. Her husband may have caught her with a lover, then beat her but had gone too far. Fearing he would be caught and charged with murder, he buried her, thinking no one would find her in the woods. Could she simply be a fallen angel? The third scenario that crossed his mind was due to her physical strength and obvious training; she could easily be an assassin that had been caught and punished. If that were the case, he needed to inform Cam as soon as he arrived. Cam would decide what should be done with her. If only she would have given him her name, where she had come from, and who attacked her. She apparently didn't feel comfortable revealing anything to him. One thing that confused him was how well spoken the lass was. By her sturdy Nordic body structure, he thought she would have had a strong Celtic accent instead of speaking proper English. She had been educated.

Even though the lass may have lost her memory, Hugh was certain she was somebody important, and he was sure someone was searching for her.

Three

Freyja approached the hearth, placed the remaining sticks from the basket over the ashes, and the fire sparked back to life. She stood, wiped her hands on her dress. Pulling what was left of her cleaning dress out to her sides, she realized besides a weapon, she needed to locate some usable clothes.

While she searched one of the small rooms in the back of the stone house, she came across some worn brown trews, a linen shirt, a tan and brown waistcoat, and a pair of knee-high boots. Quite satisfied with what she'd found, Freyja recalled Hugh had mentioned they were near Loch Morar. Hoping the loch wasn't very far, she grabbed the piece of soap she'd found and slowly opened the door. She peered out, glanced around, then crept out in search of the loch. She prayed the cold water would sooth her aching, bruised body, and wash the dirt, sweat, blood, and the awful memories away.

Lush, green rolling hills led down a gradual slope to a beach. Large sharp rocks jutted out of the silver sand, while smaller rocks dotted the shoreline. Freyja picked her way through the rocks, and settled down on a smooth, low boulder. The view was breath taking. She sat quietly for several moments and marveled at the beautiful snow-capped mountains far beyond the loch.

This place is truly heavenly, she thought.

She slipped into the fridged water. Once her tattered dress became wet, it proved quite cumbersome, though she didn't think it would be wise to remove it and bathe naked as she would have preferred. As she washed, Freyja wondered where exactly Loch Morar was, she had never heard of it before now. She had been taught to read maps; however, she didn't think she had ever viewed this particular loch on any of the maps she'd studied. She desperately needed to find a more permanent and safer place to stay. Her savior, the huge warrior, Hugh MacCormac had promised that she would be safe here, yet for how long? Truthfully, she no longer believed he would try and harm her because if he had wanted to, he could have done so anytime during the night or simply left her where he had found her. Surely, by now she would have died. Truth was, he had rescued her, provided her with shelter and with the heat of his body, kept her warm throughout the night.

Freyja shivered as the cold water crept up her back when she squatted down to rinse the soap from her hair. With only her head sticking out of the water, she turned slowly in a circle, watching for any movement along the hillside, or among the bushes and trees. Satisfied that no one was watching and waiting to attack her, she gathered her wet skirts and trudged back to shore.

The trek back to the stone house in her sodden dress was difficult. Once, safely inside the little building she secured the door, stripped herself of the wet tattered dress and hung it by the hearth. She quickly donned the clothing she'd found, then attempted to brush out her wet hair with what she hoped was a person's hairbrush and not one for a beloved dog or horse. Though most of the bristles were missing, it seemed to do a good enough job, and she was pleased to not have found any fleas living in it.

After she was dressed and her hair braided, she knew she shouldn't rely on the big warrior to return with provisions for her, which was not a problem because she could hunt and fish. Continuing her search of the hunting lodge, Freyja found a small knife, and a bow and quiver with several arrows. Even though he had left meat with her, Freyja knew she would need to find more, plus additional wood and sticks for the fire. She slipped the knife in the top of her boot and tossed the bow and quiver over her shoulder. At the door she grabbed the large, sturdy basket and ventured back outside to further investigate her surroundings and gather more provisions. It was too early to find berries; she had hoped to find heather flowers or rosehips for tea.

Birds clinging to the thin branches shared their songs as she headed down a narrow trail toward a wooded area. A red squirrel scampered across her path, chattering out a warning of her approach to other creatures in the area. Spring buds covered the trees and bushes, and once she located a shady path, the long wide branches of large ferns fanned out over the trail. Not wanting to venture too far into the forest, Freyja stayed close to the treeline and soon came across wild garlic and a few early mushrooms. She filled her basket with short sticks, tucking the thicker, longer pieces under her arm.

She smiled, suddenly spotting moss growing on the side of a tree. Now she could discern north from south and would at least know in which direction to head, whether it was dark or raining when she was strong enough and ready to leave. Other than a few islands, everything was south of Dreki Craige Castle.

If she turned to her right, she should be facing north. Ignoring the path, Freyja crept to the edge of the woods, stopped and listen for any indication of danger. After a few moments a large brown hare hopped out from behind some bushes. Slowly, she slipped an arrow from her quiver, aimed, and released the arrow. Once cleaned and dried, the hare would provide her with meat and a nice piece of fur.

After collecting the hare and her supplies, she continued north until she arrived back at the lodge. She set the items down by the door and walked toward the loch. After she scanned her surroundings, she settled down on the soft green hillside and took in the massive body of water before her. She decided when the time came to leave this place, she would follow the shoreline east, and then when she came to the end of the loch she would change her course and head north. She raked her teeth over her lower lip.

A horse would make the journey much easier.

Freyja's body ached but the thought of rosehip tea was enough to get her to stand and return to the hunting lodge. Freyja built up the fire and put water in the ewer to heat. She strolled to the bed and sat down and brushed her hand across the rough blanket.

Her thoughts quickly wandered back to the big warrior and how appealing he looked propped up on one arm upon the narrow bed. She fantasized about running her fingers through the reddish-brown curls which covered his chest and matched his beard, mustache, and the long strands of hair that hung over his shoulders. But it was the spell that those beautiful amber colored eyes generated, which caused her palms to sweat and her heart to race. She released a long sigh. Never in her life had she felt more secure and protected then when she awoke in his arms. When he sighed and affectionately pulled her back against him, his spontaneous caress had made her feel cherished. Just as quickly, that wonderful sensation morphed into being trapped and vulnerable. She'd panicked, shattering the magnificent illusion. She had waited years to be with a man and experience those feelings but under *her* terms. Now, after everything that had happened, Freyja wasn't about to ever trust a man or let herself be defenseless again.

That was not going to be a problem with Hugh MacCormac. Once he had come fully awake and she stood totally exposed and vulnerable before him, his only expression had been one of disgust and pity at her tallness and unfeminine shape. Well, that was all right with her. She would train, regain her strength, and leave here. She would get her revenge even if she died doing it.

Hugh entered the outer bailey, dismounted and handed his reins over to a stable boy. “Give him a tin of feed and a decent rubbing,” he instructed, patting the big bay’s neck. “I weel be leaving again soon.” Hugh turned and headed toward the great hall to speak with Cam about the woman he’d found yesterday. He hesitated a step and wondered if Cam would believe the lass could not recall her own name or who brutalized her. Would his cousin believe her to be an innocent victim or an assassin who’d been found out and eliminated. Or a fallen angel, beaten by a husband or lover and left to die.

As Hugh entered the keep, he heard voices coming from the great hall as people gathered for the midday meal. He strode down the corridor and into the hall. Cameron, his wife Lady Adriana, and the captain of the guards, his cousin, Malcolm Haywood, were standing by the high table. Several people in the great hall were suspiciously observing him, while others avoided making eye contact and moved away from him.

Hugh entered the keep and heard voices coming from the great hall, where people were gathered for the midday meal. He walked down the corridor into the hall. Cameron, Lady Adriana, and the captain of the guards, Malcolm Haywood, were standing by the high table. Some people in the hall watched him, while others avoided eye contact and moved away.

He realized what he must look like, moreover what he smelled like. Mayhap he should have stopped by the barracks to clean up or at least change his clothes.

Hugh caught Malcolm’s eye, and Malcolm strolled across the hall toward him. Once Malcolm reached Hugh’s side, his cousin grinned and asked, "What happened to ye?" He chuckled, then shook his head and added, "Where hae ye been all morning?"

"I donae hae time to explain now," Hugh said. "I hae an important matter to speak to Cam aboot."

"Weel, ye best make it fast." Malcolm glanced around the hall which was quickly filling up with hungry MacCormac clan members. "Auntie Moira arrived last evening and she's not alone." His eyes held a mischievous twinkle. "She has a surprise for ye. Miss Sorcha Sinclair."

"Noo isnae a good time," Hugh said, waving him off. He surveyed the head table where Cameron and Lady Adriana were now seated. He turned back to his cousin Malcolm. "I cannae speak with her noo. 'Tis most crucial I speak with Cam."

As Hugh attempted to step around Malcolm, his cousin placed a hand on Hugh's shoulder and said, "Heed my warning, cousin. Ye best crawl back beneath the rock ye slept under last night afore Auntie finds ye."

Hugh wasn't in the mood to try and decipher Malcolm's riddle, so he nodded his head and patted his cousin's shoulder in reassurance, then headed toward the high table. He'd taken only a few steps before he spotted his aunt entering the great hall. On her heels trotted a marten-sized lass with long straight black hair, alabaster skin and huge round dark eyes that appeared too large for her tiny face. Then his cousin's words echoed in his head. *"She's got a surprise for ye."* Hugh abruptly stopped in his tracks. A surprise? Och, bollox. Over the past few years his auntie had pestered him to find a decent woman to marry. Now that Cam and Adriana were married and started their wee family, Auntie Moira's attentions were focused on finding *him* a suitable wife. But marry that tiny marten-of-a-thing, he couldn't imagine it. How could his auntie possibly think *she*, a wee bairn herself, would be anywhere near a suitable wife for him?

Turning, he located Malcolm who wore an addlepated grin and nodded toward the doorway, which led to the castle's kitchen. Hugh didn't want a wife and surely not that little ghostly child his auntie had brought with her from Sinclair castle. He would rather take his chances with the brawny, fallen angel even though she'd been about to run him though with the iron poker from the hearth.

Hugh scurried toward the kitchen stairs. He sailed around the corner and nearly ran Bethany down. The maid gasped, "Hugh! I dinnae hear ye coming." She placed a hand to her chest and stepped back. "Lady Moira is searching for ye."

"So, I hae heard." He shot a quick glance over his shoulder to see if anyone had followed him. Turning back to the ladies' maid, he whispered, "Ye dinnae see me." Then paused. "Bethany, might ye hae a tin of yer wonderous healing salve ye can spare?"

She looked thoughtful for a second then asked, "Do ye need it right this moment?"

"Not immediately," he said, scratching his beard and glancing down at his unkempt clothes. "I need a bath and a change of clothes afore I ride out again."

Her eyebrows shot up, and she smiled. "I agree. I'll fetch ye a jar and will wait in the outer bailey for ye." With a sassy grin that made her eyes sparkle, she added, "That will give me a few private moments to speak with my husband Alec."

"Yer a sweet lass. I willnae be long." He slinked passed her and scampered down the steps toward the kitchen. Informing Cam of the battered lass in the hunting lodge was going to have to wait until he could return. He needed to avoid his auntie and return to the lass as quickly as possible.

Hugh slipped into the area where Maddy, the cook, who had been like a mother to him and his cousins, was busy shouting instructions to the helpers who were getting ready to serve the midday meal. The old woman turned and spotted him. She crinkled up her nose. "Och, laddie." She waved her hand in front of her nose and added, "What sort of mischief hae ye been getting yerself into?" Placing her hands on her round hips, she slowly turned her head from side to side. "Ye smell like a forgotten trout pulled from the loch."

Hugh reached out to grab and pull her close for a hug. "Come here lassie, give us a big hug and a loving kiss," he teased.

The little old woman swatted at his hands and squealed with laughter as she backed away. "Yer mad with it, and at this early in the day."

"I'm not drunk, Maddy, just starved for yer good food and a little loven." Hugh grabbed the woman and pulled her into his arms. Leaning down he rubbed his grimy cheek against hers as she shrieked and fought to get away. Loosening his hold, he planted a big loud kiss on her cheek.

"Och! 'Tis a beast yer are, Hugh MacCormac," she laughed and swatted his chest. Then reaching up, she grabbed a handful of his long hair and gave it a good yank.

"Ouch!" He yelped and frowned down at her.

"That's what ye get for harassing a defenseless old woman."

"Defenseless as a badger," he said, making a show of rubbing his sore scalp.

Waving him away, Maddy tilted back her head and chuckled. "Weel, I can only help ye with one of yer troubles, lad." She turned and gestured to the trays of food on the long prep-table. "Take what ye be needing." She wiped her hands on her stained apron and gazed up at him. "And when yer done filling yer belly, find a deep swimming whole and jump in."

"Aye." He rubbed a hand over his soiled shirt. "I could use a bath and a change of clothes, I'm thinking."

Chuckling, Maddy nodded in agreement. "Now, gather what ye want afore 'tis gone, and be on yer way."

Hugh wrapped pieces of roasted chicken, several raw vegetables, a chunk of cheese and bread in a waxcloth. He kissed the old woman on the top of her head and hurrying out the kitchen garden door. Although Corell Castle had always been his home, at that moment for some reason he felt conflicted as to where he truly belonged. He could not wait to get back to the hunting lodge to see the lass, to make sure she was alright. He needed to bathe, change his clothes, and then find suitable clothes for her.

Hugh's mind conjured up the vision of an empty lodge and his heart slammed against his ribs.

~

Hugh rode out through the main gate of Corell Castle. The supplies he'd secretly collected tied on the back of his horse. He wished he could have spoken to Cam in private, but he needed to leave as quickly as possible. He couldn't risk an impromptu reunion with his Auntie Moira. Mostly, he feared the lass would not be waiting in the hunting lodge when he returned. The thought gave him pause, and he wondered if it wouldn't be better if when he returned he found the lass had gone and the lodge empty? Nonetheless, he felt responsible for her. Until she remembered who she was and the events that led up to him finding her, and had regained her strength, she needed someone to protect her.

When Hugh was far enough away from the castle and concealed from the guards positioned on the wall, he avoided the primary trail and headed for a more remote and neglected path, which would take him along the edge of the forest and shorten his journey to the lodge. Perseus picked his way along the rocky terrain. His horse had proven his intelligence and sure-footedness more than once over the years. Perseus had even found the lass buried in the woods while he and his men were watching the underbrush for signs of an ambush.

As he trotted along the narrow path, Hugh spotted riders off in the distance. Turning his horse into the tree line, he stopped and observe them. Sixteen heavily armed Scots, a hunting party, heading east toward Loch Garry. Had he been riding on the main trail he would have ridden right toward them. Hugh didn't recognize the riders nor knew of a reason they would be riding in MacCormac territory. If they had been to Corell Castle Malcolm would have certainly informed him.

Suspicious of their purpose he crept out of the trees but stayed out of sight. He followed the riders to the edge of the MacCormac territory, then watched them continue on eastward. The group of hunters must have wandered onto MacCormac land by mistake. Now that they were gone all was well. Hugh turned back and continued on to the hunting lodge. Even though the riders were gone, a knot twisted in his guts, which sent a burning sourness to the back of his throat. Had these men been looking for the lass? Had they found her?

Hugh sank his spurs into his horse and Perseus bolted forward.

Four

It was late afternoon when Hugh finally reached the secluded hunting lodge. He heard what sounded like grunting and groaning coming from the other side of the lodge and urged his horse Perseus around the corner to investigate.

At first, Hugh wasn't sure what he was witnessing. The lass swung one of the old wooden swords that he and Cam crafted when they were mere lads as if she were fighting someone with it. The depth of the lass's concentration was marked by her tightly knit brows and intense frown. She'd donned his old brown trews, which hugged her muscular legs, a linen shirt, that hung open at her neck, and an old brown and tan waistcoat that accentuated her narrow waist. She had even found and was wearing an old pair of boots which appeared to fit her quite well. Her hair was braided and hung like a thick rope over one shoulder. Several strands had come loose and danced around her face as she practiced her sword play. A bonnier lass he'd never seen.

"Ye hae good form—for a lass," he teased.

Bollox. I should have said, fighting form. I am not here to molest the lass. I need her to trust me... To answer my questions.

After berating himself, he forced a smile and hoped it didn't look as if he were sneering.

The lass spun around to face him. And as with the poker from the hearth, she held the wooden sword pointed at him, ready to fight anything which might pose a threat to her. "Climb down off that beast and I'll show you what a *lass* can do," she said, staring blatantly up at him.

"So, 'tis yer feeling better, I'm thinking."

"Good enough to spar with you, without too much trouble." Her voice was calm, strong, with a hint of arrogance to it. Aye, she was feeling much better.

Amused and even a little eager to spar with her, Hugh replied, "I weel see to my horse and return." As he turned and rode off toward the paddock, he saw strips of meat hanging on a rod waiting to be placed over a fire, a small pelt had been cleaned and stretched between two stakes; his old bow and quiver leaned against the lodge wall. He glanced over his shoulder at the most capable and bold lass he'd ever met. After unsaddling his horse and placing him in the grassy pen, Hugh placed the items he'd brought back by the entrance to the lodge and then strolled over to her.

His eyes never left hers as he walked over to where the other sword was propped against the tree. After removing his broadsword and belt, placing them on the grass, he retrieved the wooden sword and rolled the hilt over and over in his hand as he warily approached her.

The man's sudden arrogant behavior led Freyja to wonder if he'd heard something about her and was now considering killing her. If that was his plan, she prayed his strikes would be swift and true, because she wasn't going to make it easy for him. She wasn't going to leave this world without a fight.

Freyja sidestepped, turning with him as he circled her. She needed for him to stay in front of her, if possible. Her palms were damp. All would be lost if he realized her apprehension. With a toss of her head, she flung her long braid over her shoulder and said, “You were so long in returning from the paddock, I feared you had run off. Back to the safety of your castle.”

Those serious amber eyes narrowed, and one side of his mouth raised in a boyish grin. Thin little lines appeared at the corner of his eyes. “Never fear lass.” His voice was deep and soft, like a warning growl from a large old dog, and it sent shivers up her spine. “I readily accept any and all opportunities to learn more about ye.” Mimicking her action, he gave his wild hair a toss over his shoulder. She studied the tall warrior as he swung the wooden sword before him, judging the balance and getting acquainted with the toy.

“For instance, like now,” he said, stepping closer. He bent his knees slightly and shifted his weight from one foot to the other. “Ye are a puzzle to me.” She raised her sword but held her ground. “Yer eyes,” he continued, “in the sunlight they are more green than blue. Their intent and determination to kill me...is strong. Though their assessment is unwarranted for I saved yer life, and I donae wish ye any harm. I donae think ye genuinely wish me ill either.” He continued his shrewd interrogation as he circled her.

Could it be that he was testing her to see if she would attack him or bare her soul to him like a simpering female? When he stepped to his left and dropped his right shoulder Freyja seized the opportunity and lunged forward. Her sword came down hard on his, and the crack of the two wooden blades striking each other echoed loudly in the growing silence. His arm flung out to his side leaving him open to her sword. She moved to strike, except he stepped forward, blocked her strike which caused the hilt of her sword, and her fist, to slam against his ribs. A growl and a puff of breath escaped his lips.

The sudden contact with his solid body sent a sharp pain all the way up to Freyja’s shoulder. She moaned and her sword arm dropped to her side. His strong arm seized her, wrapping around her waist and pinning her up against his hard chest.

He gazed down at her, his amber eyes drawing her in and holding her captive. His warm breath brushed across her cheek, and he muttered low and deep, "Sometime ye will hae to introduce me to the person who trained ye to fight."

Trapped and restrained in the huge warrior's arms, Freyja shoved against his chest. Instantly, he released his hold on her and took a step back. Being seized and held so tightly caused a flood of terrifying memories. Freyja's blood pounded in her ears, and she began to tremble. She needed time and space to think. She whipped the sword around to loosen the sore muscles in her arm and back. Being restrained caused her to feel trapped and angry, and trouble generally shadowed that anger.

Freyja straightened to her full height, rolled her shoulders back, and repositioned her grip on the wooden sword. She would not let her pain and exhaustion show. And she wouldn't let him trick her into revealing anything about herself to him. "When I recall his name, I will surely seek you out and inform you." When he only raised one brow, she added, "I am used to a much heavier sword than this-toy." She stared down at the wooden sword in her hand. Had she been holding her own sword and targe and not in pain from the beating she'd received, she would have shown this *man* just how well she had been trained to fight.

"Aye. Of course. 'Tis difficult to train with a toy," he replied dryly. Then pointed his sword at a pile of items on the ground by the hunting lodge and said, "I brought ye food and clothes, but I see ye found some on yer own. Maybe ye can use the jar of salve I brought ye for yer wounds."

"Oh! How very thoughtful of you," she replied sarcastically as she set her sword down against the tree and headed toward the lodge without a second glance in his direction. She had an urge to reach for his broadsword lying on the grass but knew she would need to regain all of her strength before attempting to take on this warrior. If he took offence of her touching his sword, she was sure she wouldn't live through a beating from him.

"Ye still hae not told me yer name, lass. What am I to call ye?"

"I have yet to remember my name." Then, over her shoulder as she entered the hunting lodge, she added, "You pick a name that you like, I'm sure it will be fine." Out of the corner of her eye she saw him set his wooden sword next to hers. He collected his broadsword and belt and buckled it around his waist, then picked up the pack he had brought with him which she had ignored.

~

Hugh followed her into the lodge. After the way she had attacked him, he was sure it took not one, but several men to beat her so severely that they thought her dead.

She may claim not to remember who she is or what happened, but when he'd held her close, raw fear flashed in those lovely eyes, confirming that she remembered more than she'd claimed. If there was any hope of her sharing what had happened to her, he needed to gain her trust.

After Hugh set the pack on the table, he placed his hands on his hips and said, "I hae an affection for Greek names, lass. Like Nerine, which means sea nymph, or Calista, which means most beautiful." He watched her closely. She didn't reply, just rolled her eyes at his childish game. "How about, Lotus, 'tis named after a flower and 'tis a symbol of peace." The lass forced back a smile, turned and unrolled the waxed cloth on the table. It seemed she *was* enjoying this game he'd made up.

"Despina," he continued. "It means, lady."

She abruptly turned away from the table, crossed to the hearth and placed several twigs from the basket on the glowing ashes.

"Danae," he whispered, "The woman who judges others."

She drew to attention and headed for the door. As she strutted passed him, she replied, "Whatever you wish. I better put the meat on the fire if it's to be eaten this night."

Hugh knew he hadn't come close with the names he'd suggested, something he'd said had meaning to the lass. As he picked at the items from the pack, he reviewed their sparring of words and swords. He retrieved Bethany's salve from the pack and stared at the jar. He could use some of the ointment for his own ribs where he was sure to have a goodly sized bruise tomorrow. He had sworn to be gentle with her. Yet, he hadn't wanted to be caught by the tip of even a wooden sword. He surely hadn't expected her to be so strong or able to hit so hard.

~

Freyja needed air.

What did she care if he continued to invent names until his lips fell from his face. He would never come up with her name. It was impossible. She huffed and stomped to the side of the lodge to retrieve the meat drying there. The names he had chosen, and their meanings were ridiculous. She'd never been compared to a flower or called beautiful. Yet, when he mentioned that, 'Despina meant lady' and 'Danae meant the woman who judges others,' his words were like a slap across her face. There must be more than a mere name and title that defined a person, there had to be.

She'd let the silly man have his fun but wouldn't let his words unsettle her any longer. Besides, it was going to grow dark soon, and he would leave. She wasn't sure, but she figured he would go back to Corell Castle, which he had stated was about nineteen kilometers away. He wouldn't be there underfoot, asking her more questions about her name, where she was from, and who attacked her. She needed to be alone to form a plan on how she would get back to Dreki Craige Castle to confront Finlay. Her thoughts abruptly shifted from her brother to his bloody goons, Torcall and Dunn. Why hadn't they given her the money Finlay promised and taken her to Edinburgh as he had ordered. She wondered if Finlay was even aware that she never reached Edinburgh, or that Torcall and Dunn had thought they'd killed her and disposed of her body.

She wished she had her sword and targe, her sghian dubh, or even a dirk. She felt naked without her weapons.

Freyja drew in a deep breath and then slowly released it. With her emotions once again under control, she pushed the lodge door open and entered the ancient dwelling. She found Hugh sitting at the small, worn table. He had no new questions about her name, just sat there and studied every move she made while she tended to the meat and moved around the small area. His constant scrutiny made her nervous, and worst of all, she felt defenseless. Her thoughts took her back to that horrible day in Andrew's chambers, and a queasy feeling came over her in waves. Her hands shook as she broke the bread and placed the pieces into a wooden bowl on the table for their dinner. She closed her eyes but could still envision the awful tragedy and her inability to protect Andrew. She thought of her cousin Duncan, which usually brought her joy. Today she wondered if he was safe.

Unexpectedly, the weight of a large muscular arm slipped around her shoulder, and before Freyja could stop herself, her elbow slammed sharply into the man's gut. Doubling over he gasped for breath and swore. Freyja pushed him away and hastened to the other side of the room.

"Och, lass," he huffed and struggled to straighten, holding dearly to his side. "I only meant to comfort ye. Ye seemed distraught. Ye were lost in thought and ye were trembling so, I thought ye might faint again." He ran a hand over his sore ribs. His thick brows drew tightly together as he frowned and watched her. His amber eyes darkened, and Freyja glimpsed the fierce warrior within.

"You startled me." Freyja replied, glancing away nervously

and then back to him. She raised her chin and said, "I don't like to be surprised, and I didn't faint." Before she could stop herself, she added, "For a warrior you're easily hurt."

He cleared his throat. "Ye caught me off my guard. I wasnae ready for such a jab 'tis all." He crossed to where she huddled in the corner and asked, "Do ye want to tell me what ye were thinken that upset ye so? Did ye remember something? Mayhap I can help."

What was he thinking behind those piercing amber eyes that watched her so closely. She wished she could trust him. Her mind filled with questions. Where had he gone earlier? Had he enquired if someone was offering a bounty on her? Why hadn't he taken her straight to Laird MacCormac when he had found her? What reason did he have to bring her here, when they were so close to Corell Castle? Without making eye contact Freyja meandered back to the hearth. She knew better than to assume he was honorable and would do right by her. She was quickly learning there was a large percentage of men that had no respect for any woman.

Freyja and Hugh ate their meal in silence, taking turns peering over at each other as if they expected the other to say or do something. When Hugh finished his food, he stood and abruptly thanked her for sharing what she had with him. With a wary eye, Freyja nodded her head and watched him walk out.

Confused by the lass's skittish behavior, Hugh believed it best if he bedded-down somewhere close for the night in case—something happened. He tried to tell himself that she might need him, but the thought made him laugh. The lass needed him like he needed another punch in the ribs. Frowning, he rubbed his side. Besides, it was still early evening and if he returned to Corell Castle he might run into his Auntie Moira or *"Sorcha, the small one."* To avoid them he would gladly take another punch.

Hugh made camp alongside a shallow ravine where he would go unnoticed. After making a small fire, he stretched out on the ground he stared up at the stars. He located the constellations, Leo and Virgo. While searching for The Plough, he heard a splash.

As he sprang to his feet and reached for his sword and targe, a single person broke to the surface from the water. His shoulders relaxed when he realized it was merely the lass. He watched her glide through the water and debated if he should join her or stay concealed, content to simply watch her bathe. He recalled when he and Cam were lads, how the cold water of the loch soothed their sore, bruised muscles after a day of hunting and rough games.

After a few moments, she emerged from the water naked. Her pale skin and rich honey-gold hair glowed in the soft moonlight. She pulled the wet strands over her shoulder and squeezed out the excess water. This action left a lovely view of her lush shapely backside and long muscular legs. She was quite bonnie —a goddess. Athena, the Goddess of war. Grinning, Hugh mused, *Goddess of Loch Morar*.

As she dressed and started up the path to the lodge, Hugh quickly kicked dirt over his minor fire. *Och. It wouldnae help if she saw me standing here gawking at her.*

He looked again into the night sky and beseeched Poseidon to douse his lustful body with the icy water of the loch. His cock was hard and stood out like the handle of a *halberd*. He needed to get away from the lass to think, before he did something to endanger what little trust she had in him.

Hugh gathered his things and headed toward the paddock, determined to get the vision of this bewildering woman out of his mind.

Five

Freyja awoke with a start. The faint shadows dancing outside the window confirmed the early hours before dawn. Although she was snuggled under a pile of blankets and furs she'd found in one of the other rooms, her cheeks and nose felt quite cold. She stretched, and when she rolled onto her side the muscles in her arms, back and neck screamed in pain. She cursed and moaned under her breath, wishing she had taken the time to apply the salve Hugh brought yesterday. It would have done wonders to help soothe her scrapes and bruises. Instead, she had crawled into bed and fallen fast asleep. She eyed the canister of salve and the pile of clothes and wondered if she had thanked him for the salve or his kindness. Most likely, not. Through the pain, she strained to peek at the hearth. The fire had gone out, and she would soon need to venture out from her warm bed and start a fire. She closed her eyes and snuggled further under the blankets for a few more minutes of their warmth.

When her stomach growled, she wondered if there was any food left to break her fast. She sighed, drew in a deep breath, and yawned. She couldn't put off the day much longer.

Freyja appreciated everything Hugh had done for her, but

she certainly didn't need him looking after her as if she were a child, she was perfectly capable of taking care of herself. Usually at least. She sighed. Although he had shown her nothing but kindness, she was beginning to grow weary of his constant questioning. Actually, it would be better if the big warrior never returned. The though caused her to pause. She did owe him her life, and he hadn't tried to hurt her. Freyja smiled. She liked the way his muscular body moved, the way his think auburn hair hung over his wide shoulders, and those piercing amber eyes, she would never forget the way they seemed to look right through her. She sighed. She should be thinking about getting stronger so she could leave. She had a responsibility to her clan, and to Andrew. She should be concentrating on the things that were most important, not fantasizing over the big warrior.

Her gaze floated around the tiny area and rested on the small fishing pole she'd found in the corner of the room. Later she would head down to the loch and catch a couple trout. She loved eating them, liked fishing for them, but cleaning them was not her favorite. She'd never liked touching fish or snakes. She crinkled her nose at the thought. When she was younger, she had followed her brothers down the side of the cliff to the sea and begged them to teach her how to fish.

Relaxing deeper under the covers she let memories of her childhood flow, recalling the times when both her parents were still alive and how wonderfully close her family had seemed. All was as it should have been. Each evening the family gathered in the parlor and played games and laughed, making the large parlor feel cozy and warm. Freyja missed those times. And now, Finlay had robbed any chance of them ever being a family again.

But now wasn't the time for her to get sentimental.

There were too many things that required her full attention, like healing and getting her strength back. When she was younger, Freyja had never felt she fit in anywhere until the day she held a sword for the first time. Her brothers laughed and said she would never be strong enough to fight like a man. She'd selected only the best warriors from her father's guard to train her. She'd been trained to wield a sword and a halberd, and at close quarters to defend herself with a dirk or a six-inch sghian dubh. So, after the severe beating she'd received, it was necessary to prove to herself and everyone else that she'd turned into be the warrior she'd trained so hard to become.

Throwing back the covers, Freyja got to her feet, her breath appearing in steamy white clouds. Ignoring the clean dress and soft undergarments Hugh had brought, she picked up and put on the masculine clothes from the floor next to the bed. As she fastened the waistcoat, Freyja glanced out the window toward the loch. The rising sun cast its rays across the tips of the waves, covering the water in a blanket of sparkling diamonds. She beheld the scene before her, its peacefulness in complete juxtaposition with the revenge she sought. A disturbing thought, no matter how justified that revenge was. If she returned to what had once been her home, she knew she would never be allowed to leave there alive. Now that she knew which direction was north, she would need a horse for the long journey home. She vowed that she would see justice done before being forced to leave this world. Raking her teeth over her lower lip and deliberated over just how she was going to accomplish the task.

~

Hugh was late to break his fast. When he entered the great hall at Corell Castle he found Cam and Malcolm deep in conversation at the high table. He observed the individuals who lingered, hoping to avoid his Auntie Moira and Miss Sorcha. He needed to report to Cameron and convince his laird all was well before his cousin grew suspicious of his absence and sent out a search party for him. Not seeing either his aunt or Sorcha, Hugh approached his cousins seated at the high table.

Malcolm spotted Hugh first. With a raised brow, Malcolm

nudged Cameron and said, "Och. What is this I see. It would seem our lost cousin has found his way home."

Hugh cursed under his breath. It appeared he was in for a significant amount of badgering this morning from his two cousins, who were more like brothers to him.

Cam straightened in his chair; his eyes narrowed as he swept his gaze over Hugh from the top of his head to his dusty boots. Whether it was for Hugh's benefit or for the clan members who were quietly moving closer, his cousin transformed into Laird Cameron MacCormac, better known as the fierce Black Giant. His deep growl resonated in the hushed room as he spoke. "Ye hae been absent from yer post and duties. What hae ye to say?"

Hugh stood at attention, his voice strong and clear as he replied, "My Laird has not been left unprotected." Hugh nodded his head toward the brawny guard, Big Alec, who stood not more than three feet away from the chieftain. Hugh realized that when Cam didn't turn his head, his cousin had understood that the massive warrior had taken over the duty as his shadow for the past couple of days.

With his thick black brows drawn tightly together in a frown, which matched his lips, Cam asked, "Do ye hae anything to report to me this day?"

"Aye," Hugh said, stepping forward. "I spotted sixteen Scots, a heavily armed hunting party heading east from the loch. I followed them to the territory border where they continued on."

"Were ye seen?"

"Nae. One man can sneak around unnoticed much easier than a group of warriors can." Hugh paused, when his cousin did not reply, he added, "I hae been patrolling the Eastern and Southern borders." He glanced down and brushed the dust from his leather jack. "Last eve I camped on the hill by the east end of the loch, in case they returned after it grew dark. With yer permission, my laird, I weel continue to patrol that area and report back to ye." The crowd waited to disperse until their laird nodded his approval.

"Come and break yer fast," Cam said with a wave of his hand, "'tis late and ye must be famished after all yer chasing around."

Hugh and Cam looked at Malcolm when their cousin snickered and placed his hand over his mouth undoubtedly to hide his expression due to his perverse thoughts. Hugh stepped up onto the platform, frowned and shot Malcolm a deadly look, then took the seat on Cam's right. A lad arrived with a trencher of warm sliced pheasant, cheese, and hot, flat fried bread smeared with fresh butter and placed it before Hugh. Another lad placed a mug of spiced ale and a wooden plate with two enormous berry tarts before him. Hugh glanced toward the kitchen corridor and found Maddy standing there, grinning. She untangled her hands from her apron and gave him a wave, then turned and headed back toward the kitchen. Hugh smiled to himself and dove into the delightful array of food and drink the sweet woman had saved for him.

But his feast was soon disrupted when Malcolm leaned forward and asked, "A question if I may, dear cousin, 'tis the widow McEwen's bed ye been visiting of late, aye?" Hugh paused. He rolled his eyes at his barbed-tongue cousin and shook his head.

Cam chuckled and leaned back in his chair. "Aye, 'tis said ye return at night quite late, if ye return at all." Hugh ignored their taunts and continued to eat.

"Mayhap he's prowling around the woman's quarters." Malcolm nudged Cam and grinned. "Cousin," Malcolm said. "Are ye out searching for a bonnie young maiden?"

"By the amount of food prepared so lovingly for him," Cam said, rubbing is chin pensively, "I might be want to think, our little mother hen, Maddy holds our dear lad closer to her heart than she does either of us." He turned toward Malcolm and both men chuckled.

Hugh glanced up from his food and glared at his cousins who enjoyed picking at him like a crow does a dead carcass. He wanted to join in the verbal sparring as he would normally do, but he couldn't risk a slip of the tongue and expose the lass's whereabouts. Hugh's thoughts had changed, and he figured before he told Cam about the lass in the hunting lodge, he needed to know more about her and if she had a connection to the well-armed hunting party. It wouldn't be safe for anyone if he brought her to the castle without knowing who she was or if her clan were allies or enemies to the MacCormacs. Moreover, if the clans weren't in alliance, he wasn't sure he could protect the lass against his own clan if trouble started. He had no desire to battle the lass. In fact, the thought of wrestling her to the ground conjured up images of the complete opposite.

When his plate was empty, Hugh exhaled, closed his eyes, and leaned back into his chair. He ignored his cousins' taunts and childish giggles as his mind pondered the aspect of his fallen angel's long, muscular arms and legs wrapped around him, and the sweet taste of the tender, sensitive area just below her ear. Hugh squirmed in his seat, but when his cousins' chuckling suddenly stopped, he opened his eyes and glanced around the hall in search of trouble. From the corridor by the kitchen stairs, Betheny, with her hand at her side, franticly motioned for him to come over to her. Glancing to the side, Hugh saw that both Cam and Malcolm had also noticed Bethany's gesture to him.

Hugh stood, turned to his cousins, and said, "I will report on the morrow." Cam nodded his head, and Hugh wondered at the sudden serious expressions on his cousin's face. Hugh turned and hastened across the nearly empty hall to where Bethany waited with a shy smile.

"What's amiss, lass," he asked, following her as she beckoned him further down the corridor. She stopped and glanced around Hugh toward the hall.

"'Tis Lady Moira," she whispered. "She and Miss Sorcha hae been asking where aboot ye. Malcolm informed them that ye left early this morn with a small patrol."

Even though his cousins harassed him with their teasing, it

appeared neither of them were keen on their auntie's choice of his betrothed.

Betheny guided him down the stairs toward the kitchen door, which led out to the garden. Once outside she strolled over to a patch of spring flowers. "'Tis none of my business what ye're up to, but ye should be aware that yer auntie and her shadow hae been questioning everyone aboot yer whereabouts." As she spoke, she picked purple tulips, yellow and orange daffodils, blue bells, and purple and green anemones. Hugh watched as she wrapped the bouquet with a purple lace ribbon she drew from her skirt pocket.

"There now. Isnae this pretty," she asked, handing the bouquet to him and smiling mischievously.

Hugh tentatively held the flowers, and asked, "Aye. But what am I supposed to do with these?"

Bethany wrapped her hands around his. "Every lass enjoys receiving flowers, even if for no reason. Maybe ye could find someone to give them to." She patted his hands, grinned up at him, and Hugh knew, she knew. How had she guessed about the lass at the lodge? Hugh tilted his head and sniffed at his shoulder. Could the woman smell or detect another woman on him?

"Ye best be going. Yesterday Lady Moira ventured out to the stables and quizzed the lads as to when ye were set to return. And she wasnae pleased when ye dinnae return and sup in the great hall." Grabbing him by the arms, she turned him around and gave him a gentle shove toward the gate. "Hurry now afore yer spotted. Be gone with ye." She shooed him away with both hands.

Dumbfounded, Hugh glanced over his shoulder. "Thank ye for yer diligence concerning my auntie and her latest scheme, lass. I appreciate it. I'm sorry if yer husband, Alec has been overly occupied guarding Cameron in my absence."

Bethany placed her hands on her hips and said, "Oh, Alec has taken to guarding his laird verra seriously. 'Tis a grand promotion for him to be able to take over yer duties while yer... busy."

"I weel pay him back for his assistance with this... matter."

"Donae worry. We are all behind ye. We want what and who is best for ye, and I doubt that person 'tis Miss Sorcha Sinclair." The last came in a whisper and she frowned and cast a glance around them.

"I thank ye, lass." He peered at the bouquet clutched in his callused hand, gave her a quick nod and headed for the stables. What type of reaction did Bethany expect him to receive after giving the flowers to the lass? He hoped it would be a good enough one to get the lass to reveal something about herself to him.

As Hugh came around the side of the laundry house, he caught a glimpse of Malcolm leaning up against the keep, his arms folded across his chest. More concerned with hiding the flowers from Malcolm than what his cousin was about, Hugh lowered the flowers to his side and drew out his stride, hurrying toward the stables. He slowed and listened at the open door for his aunt.

When he didn't hear any voices coming from inside, he exhaled and entered the stables. He'd witnessed firsthand how tricky women could actually be to get what they desired. He chuckled at the memories of all the crazy things Lady Adriana and sweet Bethany attempted when Lady Adriana first arrived. He hurried toward Perceus's stall and quickly collected him. Aye, he knew a woman would do almost anything if she were desperate enough.

~

The big palfrey cantered along the trail leading to the hunting lodge. Hugh's mind focused on the flowers he held, and what her reaction would be when he handed them to the lass with the rich, honey-gold hair and the deepest, blueish-green eyes. Hopefully, Bethany was correct in her theory that all lasses liked to receive flowers for no reason. Though he couldn't fathom Athena, the warrior, picking flowers and sniffing them as Bethany had, he prayed she would be touched enough to reveal herself to him without fear.

Hugh's horse slowed to a trot as he approached the hunting lodge, then veered off through the trees toward the old paddock. After placing the big horse in the pen, Hugh latched the gate and brushed the dust from the front of his clothes. As he drew closer to the lodge, he whipped his hair back over his shoulder and glanced at the bouquet of wilted and bent flowers in his hand. *Hope she appreciates the gesture.*

Hugh pushed the door to the lodge open, stepped inside and froze. The chamber, with its thick, ominous shadows appeared deserted. No coals smoldered in the hearth; everything appeared in its place as if she had never been there.

Panic stirred deep in his gut. Had the hunting party returned and taken her. Taking another step, he scanned the floor for blood, yet there weren't any signs of a struggle. He'd been a fool not to pay closer attention to his surroundings as he approached the lodge. Had he ridden over their tracks and ignored any signs? Cursing himself for letting his guard down, Hugh swung around to head back out the door. Something smashed him on top of the head. Sharp pain spread throughout his skull as the floor rushed up to meet his face.

Before he was engulfed in total darkness, Hugh heard a loud thud behind him and witnessed his old boots dash passed him and out the door.

Six

Freyja ran outside into the bright afternoon sunlight. She grabbed a sack of food and the bow and quiver of arrows from where she'd hidden them earlier. She gave a quick glance over her shoulder, making sure Hugh was not following her, then hurried down the path that led toward the paddock. The huge, bay palfrey had been unsaddled yet thankfully his headstall remained on. She hooked her provisions over the top of the fence post and decided she would forgo the heavy saddle and ride the horse bareback.

She approached the huge horse quickly but cautiously. She spoke softly, reached up and patted his neck then gathered the reins and led him over to the fence. She crawled up onto the fence, glancing once more toward the stone lodge then swung her leg over the horse's wide back. After retrieving her supplies from the fence post, she rode down the trail leading down towards the loch.

The trail soon widened, and Freyja relaxed and urged the horse into a trot. She felt guilty about hitting Hugh and taking his horse, but she had no other choice. If her life were different and she were free to travel at her leisure, she would like to investigate this area with its huge, lush, Scots pine forests and rolling hills of tall grass and silver birch trees, which swayed in the soft spring breeze. She sighed. The land around Loch Morar was truly breathtaking.

A long, sharp whistle shattered the silence. The giant bay gripped the bit between his teeth, whirled around and dashed back up the trail. Freyja pulled on the reins with all her strength, trying in vain, to get the beast to either turn or stop. Her legs hugged his sides while she grasped for a handful of the bay's black mane. With his nose stretched out straight, his ears pinned back, he ran at a full gallop, his large hooves eating up the ground beneath him. Freyja prayed she wouldn't fall. With the rough and rocky terrain, and at this pace she would surely die. The beast bolted up the hill then slid to a stop in front of the ancient, stone lodge, face to face with his angry-looking master. Frantically, Freyja kicked her heals against the bay's side and tried to pull the reins out of the man's reach. Furious, he snarled and squinted up at her. A trickle of blood dripped down the side of his face.

She swallowed hard. He was going to kill her.

Without warning, his arm reached out, and he grabbed a fist-full of clothing at Freyja's throat and yanked her from the horse and threw her to the ground. She landed with a hard thud on her back. Causing her to gasp and struggle to draw in a breath.

Standing above her, his brows protruding over his narrowed eyes, he appeared larger and fiercer than ever. Hands on his hips, a low growl slipped between his clenched teeth. "What do ye think ye were doing?" He rubbed the side of his forehead and noticed the blood on his fingertips.

"I... I didn't mean to hit you so hard."

He shook his head. "Did ye think ye would get away with knocking me senseless and stealing me horse?" His eyes closed and he released a long sigh then added more gently, "Ye should be ashamed of yerself, lass."

Freyja realized he was throwing her own words back at her.

She hesitated for a moment as her fear eased only to be replaced with pain and anger. It wasn't wise to infuriate him further, but she wasn't going to let him get away with treating her this way. "It isn't safe for me to stay here," she barked back. His frown deepened. She flipped loose strands of hair back from her face. "I cannot risk being found."

"By whom?" he asked, reaching out his hand to her. A sudden fear of how he planned to punish her for her thievery paralyzed her. Freyja stared up into his amber eyes, though his anger was still present, she sensed it was concealed behind a mystifying emotion she couldn't name.

With reluctance, she reached out. He seized her hand, his gaze never leaving hers as he easily pulled her to her feet. He didn't release her but pulled her tight up against his chest. Staring into her eyes he whispered, "I dinnae hurt ye lass, did I?"

"No." Her voice squeaked. "No more than I already am. What is one more bruise?" The gruffness in his voice vanished and suddenly a strange glint flashed in his eyes. His unexpected gentleness surprised her. She exhaled and felt her shoulders relax.

"Where did ye think ye were going?" Shifting his weight, he let their linked hands fall to their sides. She glanced away. He wouldn't understand or let her go if she revealed her plan to confront Finlay and his bloody goons.

"Lass." Her gaze swept back up to his. "I give ye my oath to protect ye, now and forever," he whispered. His sharp eyes pierced into hers, searching for the truth. "Nonetheless, ye must trust me. Tell me yer name and who might come looking for ye."

Forestalling, Freyja turned her face away and lied. "I have already told you, I cannot remember any of what happened to me in the woods that day."

His breath quickened; his massive chest expanded as he drew in a deep breath. His grip tightened on her hand, and he twisted her arm up behind her back. A whoosh of air escaped her lungs as he slammed her body up against his solid chest. Visions of Torcall and Dunn restraining her as she franticly tried to defend herself flashed in Freyja's mind. Raw panic engulfed her. She writhed against the steel trap of his arms to no avail.

The big bay tossed its head and pawed the ground.

He leaned in close, his warm breath fanning her cheek, and he snarled, "Mayhap I will take ye to Corell Castle. See how long afore yer memory returns after ye hae faced Laird Cameron."

A shiver shot up her spine, and she trembled at the thought of being presented to his chieftain, *The Black Giant*, of which she'd heard gruesome tales her whole life. Hardly loud enough to hear, she asked, "Would I be held as a prisoner there?"

"Hae ye been treated like a prisoner *here*?" He frowned. "I hae a duty to protect my laird and my clan," he said. "If a threat pursues ye while yer on MacCormac land, it becomes a threat to my people."

"I would never deliberately bring danger upon you or your clan after you saved her life. I understand and I truly admire your loyalty to your people and yer laird," she said, formidably, before continuing. "You must understand that I don't wish to bring danger or hardship upon you. This is why I must leave here before..."

He tightened his hold, glared down at her and asked, "Are ye a MacDonald, lass?"

What is he talking about? Did he mean the Glencoe MacDonalds? When she didn't reply, he whirled them both around, so the sun shined brightly upon her face.

"No! I am not a MacDonald." She struggled to move out of the blinding sun.

Jerking her around again he forced her face back into the glaring rays. "Ye are a Campbell then," he hissed.

"No!" Her head twisted from side to side.

"The MacCormac will jar yer memory for ye."

Freyja relaxed when the pressure on her arm was released, and he lowered her hand to her side. But her reprieve was short lived, for Hugh proceeded to drag her toward his horse. Was she to be delivered to Corell Castle tossed over the pommel of the horse she tried to steal, and then be judged by a monstrous beast with an army large enough to slaughter her whole clan?

She struggled to free herself from his tight grip by planting her heels in the dirt. She twisted her hand and clawed at his arm hoping to free herself from his grasp. All she received was a severe scowl over his shoulder.

Be strong, she told herself and hold your head up high. Yet she suspected if she rode into the Laird's stronghold, he would not let her ride away a free woman. Once they heard the lie that she had killed her brother, she would either hang or spend the rest of her life imprisoned in the dungeon of Corell Castle, or worse, she'd be returned to Dreki Craige Castle in shackles to face Finlay.

Boiling acid of pure panic bubbled up inside her and before she could stop herself, she pulled back and shouted, "My name is Freyja Rasmusdatter."

What have I done?

~

Hugh whirled around to face her, then suddenly released his hold on her. Expecting her to continue with her charade of not remembering anything, he was surprised she spat out a name. She pulled her shoulders back and lifted her chin as if challenging him while trying to hide the fact that her body whole trembled with trepidation.

The tall brawny lass stood before him dressed in his old worn and tattered clothing, her thick braid hung forward over one shoulder. He watched as she pulled her shoulders back and lifted her chin in an attempt to gain some sense of control of the situation.

"What did ye say?"

"My name is Freyja Rasmusdatter," the lass said with conviction.

Rasmusdatter. Aye, the lass could verra well be the daughter of a Norseman. Yet, Hugh had never heard tell of a Norseman in their area called Rasmus. Furthermore, one who sired a daughter and educated her so, to speak the King's English perfectly.

He respected the lass's sense of pride and determination but reminded himself that it was in her Norse blood to fight him to gain power. Now that he had broken through her tough exterior, he needed to show her respect if he wanted answers.

"Come," she said, turning away from him and entering the lodge. "Let me tend your wound. I will make a tea to help dull your aching thick skull."

Hugh saw a glimpse of a smile before she turned away. He followed her into the lodge; he would grant her this victory. They both stopped and surveyed the broken bowl and flowers scattered across the stone floor. She bent down and proceeded to pick up the pieces of pottery. Though his head pounded from where the pot made contact, his pride hurt worse for letting her get the best on him, than from the lump growing on top of this head. He'd been a fool to think bringing the lass flowers would place him in her good graces. "Let me lass, I mean, Freyja." Hugh reached out to help her up, but she ignored his hand and stood.

"I'll start the tea," she replied in a rigid voice as she crossed to the pot on the swey. She poured water into the pot and swung the swey over the coals. She stirred the coals and placed more wood on the embers. "Sit and let me tend to your head."

Hugh tossed the remnants of the pot and the dried and bent flowers into the corner, then settled at the table. Holding a piece of cloth and the salve he'd brought for her wounds and bruises; the lass approached him. She paused before setting the items on the table.

"I will not hurt ye, Freyja." Hugh glanced up and when she appeared to relax, he continued, "and I'm sorry if I hurt ye when I pulled ye from my horse."

She nodded her head and placed the jar on the table. The cloth was cold and damp and felt good on the cut as she gently wiped the blood away. "I'm sorry..." She paused. "I shouldn't have hit you so hard, but I know from experience that warriors have very thick skulls."

Hugh glanced at her briefly and then smiled as he noticed her effort to refrain from laughing aloud after her second insult about his thick skull. She put her rag down and opened the jar of salve. "I don't know what's in this jar, hopefully it will not sting too terribly." She dabbed a little on the open wound and when he didn't move she placed a little more. After she wiped her hands on the cloth, she returned to the swey at the hearth and poured the hot water into two mugs. He could smell the mixture of nettles and wood sorrel, as she carried the mugs over to the table. Before offering him the healing tea, she deliberately took a sip, which he figured was to prove she hadn't added anything harmful to his mug.

"My thanks, Freyja." He gestured to the other chair. "Please sit." Hugh sipped his tea. "I like the tangy lemony flavor of the wood sorrel."

The lass nodded her head as she sat. She sipped her tea, which would help heal her wounds and sore muscles, too.

What a mess we both are.

Hugh rested his arms on the table and asked, "Can ye tell me what happened to ye, and how ye ended up in such a predicament?"

Her gaze caught his and with a pinch of sarcasm, she said, "Ye mean, *situation*?" Then she glanced down at her mug, twisting it around as if wondering how to answer him. After a moment she replied faintly, "I wish I knew why all of this happened. How people can do such things to others."

When she wasn't being a warrior for which she'd been trained, the lass was thoughtful and vulnerable. Of course, she would not appreciate him pointing those facts out to her, so he changed his tactics.

"Freyja, the Norse goddess of love, beauty, and fertility. It suits ye," he stated light heartedly, hoping to make the atmosphere lighter.

She blushed at his comment but didn't reply.

"Old Norse mythology claims that Freyja rode through the heavens in an elaborate carriage. She selected only the most exceptional fallen warriors from the battlefield, leaving the other warriors for Odin to take back to Valhalla."

She peered up, and Hugh sensed her skepticism.

"Freyja, are ye married?"

Shaking her head she replied, "No."

"Are ye certain?"

"I think I would remember something that important."

"Do ye hae any family?"

She glanced down at her hands, then slowly shook her head from side to side.

Hugh felt the sadness he saw in her eyes and wondered what had happened to her family. She apparently lived in a constant state of fear, but of whom she would not tell him. He wondered if the poor lass had suffered so much that she feared everyone.

Seven

The warm spring morning wasn't wasted on Hugh, spring offered clear skies and the promise of new beginnings. As he returned from Corell Castle, he rode up to the paddock by the hunting lodge and dismounted. He put the two horses in the fenced in area, collected some items from his pack and headed toward the lodge. He had awoken early from his campsite by the ravine and rode to the castle for more supplies, and a couple of surprises he hoped Freyja would enjoy.

After her attack on him yesterday, then witnessing her fear, and her persistent claim that she could not remember what had happened to her, Hugh had spent the night worrying about what she might do in a moment of panic. But once he had fallen asleep his dreams were overrun with detailed visions of Freyja in his arms. After awaking this morning, he concluded the lass needed someone to protect and to provide for her. Scratching his chin, he'd never thought himself the type of man who would take on such an undertaking. He was a warrior; his laird's second in command. What changes would occur to his way of life if he took responsibility for her? Nonetheless, he would first need to speak with Cam and get his approval.

He sprinted up to the lodge, knocked once and opened the door. The ancient stone structure appeared empty. A tightness seized his chest at the thought that something might have happened to her. But with no evident sign of a struggle, his suspicion quickly changed to anger as he realized she might have simply left on foot.

Hugh trudged out of the lodge, searching the ground for footprints. He followed the one set of prints that led down the path to the loch. Halfway down the trail he caught a movement out of the corner of his eye and stopped and stared. Like a mythical sea creature, she sat perched naked upon a large rock out in the loch with the sun glistening off her long honey-blonde hair. She glanced up, noticed him, and like a beautiful siren of the sea, she dove into the water.

Hugh watched for her to reappear. After several moments passed and she hadn't surfaced, Hugh raced down the trail toward the beach. He stripped off his clothes and plunged into the water. Surfacing, he whipped his hair back from his face and looked around. Without warning, Freyja appeared in front of him. She glanced up and smiled impishly as if she had played a trick on him.

He reached out, grasped her arms and pulled her to him. Her hands pressed against his arms, and her pebble-hard nipples brushed against his chest. Her greenish-blue eyes stared up at him with anticipation. The intense feelings he had for this mysterious woman where all new to him. Leaning forward, he wrapped her in his arms and kissed her long and hard. He didn't care about any other men she'd lain with; he wanted Freyja to be his woman. He wondered how Cam and his aunt would receive this wild creature when he brought her back to Corell Castle with him. Once she was at the castle and under his protection, she would be safe from whoever attacked and beat her, plus she would be closely guarded if they chose to come looking for her.

She pushed him away. "Please," she panted, "you need to stop."

"Do ye no like kissing and touching," he teased as he brushed his thumb lightly across her shoulder blade. She sighed and gave him a strange look. He moved closer and said, "Ye donae fancy love or a romantic entanglement, lass?" He enjoyed teasing her, watching the warrior in her turn into a gentle woman and blush.

"Romance is for fools," she replied bitterly and tried to turn away from him. "And I have no time for such foolishness. What is important to me is to heal and then spent every moment training, so I can defend myself." He pondered her remark. She shrugged and said, "Besides, love, itself, is a waste of time. It isn't real; it's something fools and poets wax on about."

"Oh, lass, this is where yer wrong." Had she never experienced love, kindness or affection from the members of her family? Hugh knew the anguish from the absence of immediate family. His chest tightened with empathy, and he pulled her close. "Love between a lad and lassie can be quite pleasing. Kissing and touching, whispering tender words that arouse." Her hands slid up his arms as he pulled her up against him. "'Tis a chance to learn all aboot what the other wants to hear and all the secret places they desire to be touched. How they want to be caressed and kissed." He kissed her neck, nibbled her tender earlobe lightly, then whispering, "Discovering each other's intimate desires and dreams."

Freyja's head tilted to the side, surrendering to his hot lips. The sensations he caused took her breath away, and she knew she shouldn't let this happen. It was only one of those *romantic entanglements* he'd mentioned. It wasn't love. It wasn't the feelings that lasted a lifetime. That sort of love only existed in fairytales. Most marriages were not love matches. She cursed herself. She wanted real love, or she didn't want anything at all. Her thoughts rolled back in her mind to her parents, and the way her father had treated her mother. How he had no time to visit her death bed and how quickly he returned to his whoring ways the same day her mother passed. Her brothers display of affection had not been much better toward the maids they occupied themselves with.

She pushed away from him. "I have no aspirations about love. I only wish to regain my strength and move on with my life." She frowned; she needed to concentrate on revenge, not on the gorgeous naked man before her. Yet, she couldn't help herself. She enjoyed how his soft auburn curls that covered his broad muscular chest tickled her breasts. Freyja recalled how warm, content, and secure she felt when she awoke wrapped in his arms. How those same curls felt against her back.

Hugh's eyes filled with a boyish mischief, and he said, "I brought ye a horse. I thought ye might enjoy a ride along the loch today."

"What!" Had she heard him correctly. "You brought me a horse?"

"Aye, lass. I hope ye like her."

He gripped her arm and helped her to shore. As the water became shallower, Freyja tried to look away, but his bronzed, warriors' body was perfect, and she couldn't help herself. He wrapped his plaid around her, then pulled on his shirt. Freyja paused and glanced around looking for any signs of danger. Only after she was convinced they were alone, she led the way up the trail to the lodge.

Once they entered the stone building, she slipped the plaid from her shoulders and let it fall. She stood naked before him. "Ye hae the body of a goddess, lass. How men must worship ye and want ye for their own." He pulled her close and gently kissed her neck and along her shoulder. His hands slowly slid down over her hips, and he drew her closer.

Freyja was quickly losing the battle of restraint. Her sense of reasoning washed away by his kisses and the thought of what he could possibly teach her. One large, calloused hand slid up her spine to the long column of her neck then into her hair. His lips found hers again and his kiss was gentle and inviting. Freyja wrapped her arms around his neck, pressed her naked body to his, and deepened the kiss. His tongue slipped into her mouth, dancing over and around her tongue, teasing it to mimic his motions as his hands caressed her back and hips. He sucked her tongue deep into his mouth and crushed her body tightly to his.

The sudden possessiveness in his demeanor jerked Freyja back to reality and she pushed him away. His amber eyes had turned black; his expression wavered between lust and danger. Though with this man she wasn't certain they were not the same thing.

Her heart pounded wildly. She glanced up at him through her thick lashes and said, "I thought you wanted to take me for a ride?"

One corner of his mouth lifted in a smirk. Then he placed his forehead against hers and whispered in a strained voice, "Aye, lassie. 'Twas foremost in my mind." He released her.

They both dressed and Hugh grinned as he turned and observed the lass before him. He'd become accustomed to seeing her in his old clothes and boots. If he recalled, they hadn't fit quite the same or looked as good on him as they did on her. Before they left the lodge to ride the horses, he crossed to Freyja. "Can ye be trusted not to ride off or attempt to cut me down, lass?"

Her brows pulled together as she stared at him. He wanted to reach out and smooth the fine lines that appeared along her forehead. Then she snickered and said, "I'm in no position to make any long-term promises, but I assure you I will not ride off or attempt to harm you in any manner, this day."

"I appreciate yer honesty," he said, and pulled his hand out from behind his back and handed her a backsword and belt he'd brought with him for her. Her lovely eyes grew large and round, and she took the sword and buckled the belt around her waist.

Her sweet lips opened, and she drew her lower lip into her mouth. He was fascinated when her perfect white teeth raked over her lower lip as she examined the backsword. Then her expression grew serious, and after a moment she asked, "Is this truly for me?"

"Aye. As long as ye donae use it against me."

"Your generosity means so much to me, and since you have sworn to protect me, I feel honor-bound to swear my fealty to you." She took a deep breath and stated, "I vow that I shall never turn against you or attempt to take your life."

Her pledge surprised and pleased him. Placing his finger under her chin, he tilted her head back and kissed her. Then he took her hand and led her out of the lodge toward the paddock where the two horses grazed.

However, once outside, Freyja slowed. She glanced from side to side, checking her surroundings, and surveying the area as if she expected danger lurked behind every rock and bush. She was tense and alert, and her lush lips were pulled tight in a thin flat line. As she walked, she rested her hand on the hilt of the sword. There was even a touch of apprehension in those beautiful eyes of hers. Yet, that all changed when they neared the paddock. Freyja admired the dapple-grey mare who raised her head as they approached.

"She is aboot six years old. Her name is Saga, which means, *to see*. 'Tis said this little mare can predict the future and is able to foresee danger."

"She's beautiful," Freyja whispered. The mare ambled to the fence and lifted her head over the top rail.

Hugh chuckled and pulled an apple from his pocket and handed it to Freyja. "She is looking for a treat. She's verra gentle," he added as Freyja took the apple from him and with her bare hands, snap it in half, then in quarters. She spoke quietly as she offered the mare one piece at a time.

"I assumed ye preferred to ride bareback," he said, walking away. "But I thought ye might want to try a saddle this day."

Freyja ignored his teasing about her earlier attempt to escape and crawled between the fence rails into the paddock. The mare nuzzled her for the last piece of the apple. The mare's persistence reminded Freyja of the mare she favored at home. She leaned down and grabbed a handful of dried grass and swept it along the mare's neck and across her back. Hugh had saddled his horse and was now tying a pack across the back. Freyja threw the saddle up onto Saga's back and secured the leather straps. Next, she grabbed the bridle, and Saga lowered her head so she could slip it on.

She followed Hugh out of the paddock and down the trail in the direction of the loch and rode along the water's edge in silence. Finally feeling at peace, Freyja exhaled and relaxed. She had a sword at her side, a knife she'd found in the lodge tucked into her boot, and a horse beneath her. The weather was perfect. The morning had been especially perfect when Hugh surprised her by joining her in the loch. She smiled to herself as visions of his braw, naked body materialized in her mind. Everything would be perfect if they could be left alone without fear of being hunted down.

As if he knew she'd been thinking of him, Hugh glanced over his shoulder, grinned, and said, "Since ye dinnae fall from Perseus to yer death, I ken ye must be a fair rider."

The trail ended and a field of tall grass stretched out before her. Freyja wasn't about to let the opportunity to show him just how well she could ride, slip by. She leaned forward, Saga's ears twitched, and Freyja sunk her heels into the mare's sides. "Fair," she yelled as she and Saga shot past Hugh and raced across the open field. The mare was fast and surefooted; her long black mane whipped in the wind. It wasn't long before she heard the thundering hooves of the big bay palfrey coming up beside her. Hugh's long auburn hair whipped in the wind behind him. The devil wore that boyish grin which made her heart pound wildly.

They flew across the field, slowing only when they reached the edge of the forest. Freyja reined in her horse, stopped, then turned to face Hugh. Laughing, she said, "That was fantastic. I haven't felt so free in weeks. You were right, this delightful lady has a smooth gait." She leaned forward and padded the horse's neck.

"I thought ye would make a good match," Hugh said, stroking his horse's thick neck. The big bay tossed his head and pranced in place. "Enough, Perseus." He scolded his horse good-naturedly.

"Why did you name him Perseus," Freyja asked, wanting to know more about the man and his huge beast of a horse. As far as she knew Palfreys were generally not as tall as this one.

"He is named after the greatest hero of Greek mythology. Perseus was the son of Zeus and the mortal Danae." He sat proudly atop the majestic bay with its long black mane and tail and spoke as if he were speaking about a close friend. "He was especially known for slaying the fearsome Gorgon monster, Medusa."

"I remember studying about King Poly...," she paused for a moment, "I can't recall his name, but didn't he send Perseus on a quest to kill Medusa and bring back her head? And while the lad was gone, the king planned to force Perseus's mother to marry him?"

"Aye, lass. Ye're quite right. King Polydectes considered Perseus as an obstacle which kept Danae from marrying him, so he sent the lad on a mission he figured Perseus would never return from." Hugh dismounted. "There is a trail here that will take us to a stream where we can water the horses."

Freyja dismounted and stretched. Her ribs, side, and back still hurt, even though the bruising had started to change to a greenish-yellow color. She straightened and found Hugh staring at her. His expression seemed so peculiar, she couldn't imagine what he was thinking. He exhaled and asked, "Are ye all right lass?"

"I'm quite all right," she replied, "just a little stiff. Lead on. I will follow you."

He headed toward a narrow trail that led into a dense forest of giant pines. Large ferns and leafy bushes covered the ground on both sides of the trail. The thick canape above them offered shade, which caused a much cooler temperature and a dampness in the woods. The dank earthy smell took her back to a day in a much similar woods. The day Torcall and Dunn beat her and left her to die. A shiver slithered up Freyja's spine. She needed a distraction from the evil that plagued her each day. "Tell me more about your Greek hero, Perseus."

Hugh's eyes sparked with enthusiasm. "Weel," he started in a strong voice. "King Polydectes dinnae know the other gods that dinnae like him were going to help the lad. God Hermes gave Perseus a curved sword and a pair of winged sandals. The goddess Athena gave him a mirror of polished bronze and a cap from Hades that had the power to make oneself invisible."

A hat that could turn you invisible sounded like something Freyja should have owned. It would have come in dandy more than once in her past.

"Perseus found the cave that Medusa lived in. Since he wore the invisible cap and winged sandals, he was able to fly into her cave and find her sleeping. To avoid looking at her else he would turn to stone, Perseus looked at her reflection in the mirror Athena had given him and he cut off her head with the sword from Hermes."

Freyja marveled at the story and at Hugh's contagious enthusiasm. "What a wonderful story. Thank you for sharing it with me," she said as he stopped by a fast-moving, narrow stream to let his horse drink.

One corner of his mouth hiked up in that boyish grin of his. "'Tis not finished yet. Perseus thought he had killed the Gorgon by cutting off her head, but after doing so, the head retained its ability to turn onlookers to stone. Perseus flew back to Seriphos, where his mother was being forced into marriage with King Polydectes. Using the head as a weapon, Perseus proved that he was not only a god but a true warrior and not afraid to confront his enemies. Perseus then turned the king into stone and saved his mother."

His deep voice held her captive, though when he smiled, his boyish charm reassured Freyja she had no reason to fear the huge warrior. She coaxed the grey mare closer until Saga stepped over the steep rocky edge into the stream and drank. "You must have had a good tutor and enjoyed your studies to remember all of that story."

He nodded his head, his eyes studying the ground as if contemplating something from his past. "Cam hated being forced to stay inside to study. Ye couldnae get the lad to read, so once we were alone, I would tell the stories to him, sometimes I even used silly voices to keep his interest."

Freyja stared off into the distance and thought back to the elderly Englishmen who came to teach Laird Weir's three wild children. Andrew and Finlay played tricks on Mr. Hallingsworth daily, but Freyja enjoyed reading and learning new things. He instilled confidence in her and often told her how intelligent she was. He also stated that due to her strong sense of fairness and morality, it made her more acceptable to take over as chieftain of clan Weir than her brothers. That dream had died along with all her other dreams. "It sounds like you did your cousin a great service." She turned when Saga stepped back up onto the bank.

"Come," Hugh said, leading his horse further up the trail.

Freyja gather her reins and trailed behind him. The dense forest and landscape here with its streams, bushes, and scattered rocks, were so different from the stark flat rocky land and cliffs of the far north. Here you were surrounded in a sea of greenery. At Dreki Craige Castle you could actually stand on the north cliff, on the edge of the world, and you could see out across the sea forever. Nothing compared to its vastness or the mysteries beyond.

The thought of never returning home without being imprisoned or hanged, caused Freyja's heart to ache. She missed everyone who worked in the castle, the stable master and the stable boys. She'd been forced to leave her favorite cousin

Duncan and all her kinsman and many friends without being allowed to proclaim her innocents or the say any words of farewell.

Freyja vowed she would return to Dreki Craige Castle and confront Finlay and proclaim her innocence to her clan. Like Perseus, she'd prove herself a true warrior, and not afraid to stand before or challenge her enemies.

Eight

The sun sank low in the westerly sky as Freyja and Hugh rode in amicable silence easterly toward the hunting lodge. Freyja reveled in the freedom and the simple joy of riding next to Hugh as his equal. They meandered their way up a steep trail to the crest of a large hill. Hugh whirled his horse around and stopped and stared past Freyja back toward the west. Seeing the awe struck look on his face, she feared they were being followed and quickly reined in the mare next to him. Like a large ball of fire, they sat quietly for several moments and watched the sun slowly descended into the sea. This wasn't the first sunset Freyja had ever seen. It felt as if she was seeing the sunset for the first time through Hugh's eyes, making the moment extra special.

"'Tis as if an artist painted a scene of the sea," he whispered, "then decided the picture looked the same as his other paintings. That it needed more color; thus, he passionately washed the clouds, the sky, and sea in pink, orange, and purple. The result —a masterpiece."

Hugh turned; his contemplative expression revealed yet another side of his character, a side she found intriguing.

"I didn't realize we were so close to the sea. It's breathtaking." Exhaling, she relaxed and admired the magnificent view of the setting sun and the extraordinary man beside her.

"'Tis late and I could eat a good-sized calf," Hugh said as he rubbed his flat stomach. Freyja smiled and let her horse fall into step beside his. Hugh laughed and flashed her a wide grin. "Once when we were lads aboot nine or ten, Maddy had spent the whole day baking sweets for a celebration. The sweets, mind you, were to last for several days," he chuckled. "Weel, after Maddy had gone to her bed, Malcolm, Cam and I snuck into the kitchen, quiet as mice, and raided the larder. We ate all the biscuits before moving onto the tarts, then devoured several custard pies and a roasted turkey by the morning." He rubbed his belly as if he could still taste the feast.

Both amused and horrified by his tale, Freyja couldn't help but laugh, and then asked, "What happened? Did you get sick? Were you caught?" If she ever returned home, she would retell his stories to Duncan.

"Aye. Cam and I were sick as pups who'd eaten their first turtle." Freyja cringed at the thought. "Och, but not Malcolm. The wee bastert could eat as much as Cam and me together and never get sick. The *wee bam* vanished before Maddy found us the next morning sprawled out in what wouldnae stay put in our gullets. Seeing we were still alive, she recited every swear word she knew in Celtic, and a few we were sure she had made up."

"Oh, how terrible. What a mess that must have been. Did she make you clean it up?"

"No, but that would hae been more desirable," he said, becoming very serious. "Our sweet, dear, Maddy, who had been like a mother to us, made the two of us stand in the great hall afore the evening meal and sing a song that she sang to each of us when we were mere nurslings as loud as we could, whilst Malcomb, the devil, watched and laughed."

Freyja covered her mouth trying to hide her laughter, and tears stung her eyes as she pictured the two sick lads singing their punishment before their clansmen. He looked pitiful and shook his head and as if he did not believe his own tale. "Well, did you learn your lesson to stay out of her larder?"

"As we grew older and broader, sweet little Maddy seemed to anticipate our arrival, and ever since that day she has had food ready at any time of the day or night." He grinned triumphantly.

"I imagine you three got into quite a bit of trouble growing up."

"Weel, not too much trouble," he said with a wink. "Though one time, I think we were aboot ten and three, therefore Malcolm would've been aboot ten. We lined our horses up for a race, then crawled up on their backs and stood. The goal was to race side-by-side around the list and see which one would be the last man still standing."

These three lads were worse than her two brothers. "What happened? Who won the race?"

"Cam counted to three and we yelled for the horses the run. We didn't get too far afore Malcolm fell and broke his arm. Cam's horse and mine stayed next to each other until several guards showed up and stopped us. We were never allowed to finish the race, yet we agreed we'd race again someday to settle which of us was the better horsemen." His gaze locked with Freyja's, and he gifted her with his lopsided boyish grin she was sure got him into and out of trouble more than once over the years.

"You and your cousins seem to have had a lot of wild adventures. Do you have any brothers or sisters," she asked, thinking how fun it would have been to grow up with Hugh and his cousins in this wonderful part of the country.

Hugh rode in silence, and Freyja worried she had touched on a subject he was hesitant to speak of. After a few moments, Hugh said, "I had a younger brother, Robert. He traveled a lot with my father. On a returning trip, they were attacked, and my father and brother were both killed."

"Oh, Hugh. I am so sorry. I didn't mean to pry or cause you to recall such a painful memory."

He turned his head and smiled. "Ye may ask me anything ye wish, Freyja. 'Twas a long time ago."

Suddenly, she wanted to know everything about this man who saved her life, who made her feel things she had never before felt for a man. There were so many sides to him it seemed, and she wanted to know everyone.

"What about your mother, is she still living?" Freyja immediately regretted asking him something so personal. She raked her teeth over her lower lip while she waited for his answer.

Hugh glanced at her and then away. Staring straight ahead he said, "She died a short time after my father and brother were killed. I think she died of a broken heart. My Auntie Moira came and helped raise me."

Not much louder than a whisper, she said, "I am truly sorry, yet I understand how that could happen." Freyja missed her mother even after all these years. And Andrew, though he hadn't shown her much affection, he had at least been civil to her.

They reached the paddock and unsaddled the horses. Freyja wiped Saga down with dried grass as Hugh filled two pails with water. He cut a large bundle of tall grass and tossed it over the fence into the paddock. Though she was tired, she didn't want the day to end. After everything they had shared that day, she knew it would be difficult to walk away from him when the time came for her to leave.

"Are ye asleep where ye stand?" Hugh asked, strolling up to her.

Freyja exhaled. "No, just thinking."

"Ye best get yer rest, lass. It has been a long day. We should hae returned earlier. I will camp by the ravine again."

Freyja placed her hands against his chest and gazed up into his dark eyes. "Thank you for today. I haven't felt this happy for a long time."

Hugh ran his fingers through the strands of hair that had

come loose from her braid. He toyed with a lock which curled around his finger, then leaned forward and gently kissed her lips. Without a word, he turned and walked away, disappearing into the trees.

After changing out of her clothes and washing up, Freyja slipped her shift over her head. Her heart was heavy with guilt. After everything Hugh had shared with her about his life, Freyja knew she needed to tell him the truth about what had happened to her. Instead of braiding her hair for bed, she brushed it out, pulled it back and tied it with the purple ribbon, which had been tied around the flowers Hugh had brought her. Though the flowers were now crumpled and broken, she had kept the purple ribbon and would treasure it forever.

In her shift and barefooted, Freyja opened the door and crept out into the night. In the distance she could see the glow of Hugh's fire. She headed toward his camp, prepared to confess everything to him this night. Hopefully, he would understand why she had lied to him and forgive her.

Hugh leaned back against a tree. He snapped a twig into pieces as he stared into the flames of the fire and reflected on the things he'd discovered about the lass today. She was starting to trust him and, in the moments she let her guard down ever so slightly, she'd inadvertently revealed a little about herself.

She'd stated she hadn't felt happy or free in weeks, which indicated she remembered being pursued and brutally beaten. She had also remembered studying about King Polydectes, although she hadn't been able to recall his name, she knew the tale of Perseus's quest to kill Medusa and bring back her head. A sign that she was obviously well educated. All of the small details were starting to give Hugh a picture of Freyja, although it was still fragmented and distorted like the shattered pot she'd hit him with. The detail that gnawed at him the most though, came when he'd spoken of the death of his father and brother, and his mother's passing, a sadness had crept across her face revealing some deep hurt. She'd told him she had no family, which he hadn't fully believed. However, now he was convinced she had no family that loved her or would protect her.

His mind flooded with questions. How many men had hurt her? Had she been in their possession and escaped? If so, how long had they pursued her before they finally caught and beat her, and left her for dead?

Furthermore, if she was supposed to be dead, who did she think was after her?

Hugh heard the crinkling of leaves underfoot and pulled a dirk from his boot. He glanced up as Freyja glided out of the trees and sauntered toward him. She stood before him completely illuminated by the fire behind her. Her long, shapely body fully visible through her thin shift. Drawing in a ragged breath, Hugh whispered, "Ye are truly a goddess, lass." His heart raced, his blood boiled in his veins, and he feared the vision would vanish if he moved.

"I have come to talk to you," she said hesitantly. She shivered and wrapped her arms around herself.

"'Tis late and I hae no words left. I talked more this day than ever before." He chuckled and could think of more enjoyable things to do with her right then besides talking. "Come, yer trembling," he said, opening his plaid, offering her a place to sit and the warmth of his body.

Freyja hesitated for a second, then knelt down and cuddled up next to him. He wrapped his plaid around her shoulders and pulled her up against his side. "Better now?"

Her hand timidly brushed across his chest. The flames of the fire revealed raw passion in her eyes. "Your body is on fire." She snuggled closer.

"Aye, ye do that to me, Freyja." He leaned down and kissed her. Her arms slipped up and clamped around his neck. Hugh glided a hand into her thick hair, freeing it from the ribbon, and deepened the kiss.

Freyja's leg moved between his. She pushed him back until he stretched out on the ground beneath her, and she sprawled on top of him. Surprised but intrigued by her eagerness, Hugh let her take the lead, set the pace. She rolled around and covered his neck and face with frantic kisses. She bit his chin twice, and when she pulled his hair with aggressive force, he grabbed her arms and flipped her over onto her back. "Easy now lass. I donae wish to be rough with ye. There is no need to rush, we hae all night." He leaned down to kiss her, just as she reared up to meet him, one hand grabbing his hair again. Hugh grasped her wrists, stretched her arms out wide and held them down. The lass was clearly used to a rough hand, and Hugh appreciated a woman who wouldn't lose her nerve and cry and shy away because of his size. Nevertheless, he still wanted Freyja's trust, so he would save the brawling for another time.

"Hush now, be still." He leaned forward and gently kissed her, then ran his tongue over her lower lip. He kissed her neck and licked her earlobe.

Freyja watched his every move with a mixture of fear and anticipation. He worked his way lower to the swells of her breasts. Drawing one hard pebbled tip into his mouth, he suckled her through her thin shift, and she bucked beneath him. Cautiously, he let one of her arms go and stretched out beside her.

His hand slid down her side and under her shift and up her long, shapely leg.

Freyja was definitely in over her head. She strived and fought to control herself. Struggling with the feelings of pleasure coursing through her body and the uncertainty of what to do next. She had never stayed around and watched what all happened between her brothers and the maids. She'd only witnessed the wrestling, biting, and hair-pulling before. Now she didn't know what she was supposed to do.

"That's a good lass," he said, drawing her nipple back into his mouth. He moved his hand tentatively over her hip and stomach and lower until he found her most secret place. His hand teased and rubbed the sensitive area until she gasped and feared she was going to swoon. Bracing himself above her he nudged her legs apart and slowly pushed himself against her. Instinctively, Freyja bucked beneath him. Her hand flew up and grasped his shoulders to help keep her grounded.

Hugh plunged into the lass; she was so wonderfully tight. He drew back then thrusted again, then stopped, confused at hitting a barrier.

"Don't stop," she pleaded, thrusting her hips toward him.

"Lass, are ye sure?"

"Yes. please. Don't stop."

He thrust again and again until he was buried deep within her and spent. "I hope I dinnae hurt ye. Why did ye not tell me yer were a virgin?"

"What made you think I was not a virgin?" she asked, pushing his weight off her.

"I had thought that ye might be a fallen angel. That mayhap yer husband or lover was the mon who beat ye." She turned away from him. "But I thank ye for giving me such a special gift," Hugh said, pulling her close, so her head rested on his chest and wrapped his plaid around them. "Sleep now lass, we'll talk more tomorrow."

Hugh lay awake staring into the flames of the fire. Had she acted so wild because she knew what was about to happen or because she hadn't known what was about to happen? He smiled and pulled her closer. He didn't care; he liked when his women were enthusiastic.

How wonderful it would be to stay at the hunting lodge with Freyja alone forever. Yet, he had already taken too much time away from his duties. He would take her with him when he returned to Corell Castle in the morning. She would be safer there. And after he spoke to Cameron and procured his consent, he would inform Freyja that they would be married.

Nine

Eager and apprehensive about meeting his clan and the people he'd told her about; Freyja nudged her mare to stay close to Hugh as she followed him. She glanced around trying to memorize her surroundings. She wanted to make sure that if the time for her to leave came during the middle of the night, she would be able to find her way back to the stone lodge. From there she would head north.

That morning, Hugh had awakened in a bad temper and Freyja couldn't help but wonder if she had done something wrong during their coupling the night before. She had wanted to please him, except her knowledge of what went on between a woman and a man was limited. Once when she was younger and had been picking berries in the woods, her brother Finlay had dragged one of the maids into the thick grove of trees near her. She waited, silently, for a short while, spying on the two just long enough to see their passionate activity get started. She hadn't observed them for very long, but those moments stuck in her memory. Last night she wished she had stayed longer; the education she would have received would have been quite helpful in pleasing Hugh. She had tried to mimic the maids' actions and even though, she was inexperienced, she thought she had done quite well. Except this morning, Hugh curtly informed her that he needed to return to his duties at the castle, and he had decided she would be much safer staying there. She disagreed with him for several minutes, then realized there was no use trying to change his mind. If there was anything she had learned over the years, it was that you couldn't reason with men because of their thick skulls and tiny brains.

She pushed her horse up next to Hugh's. They rode in silence, Hugh speaking only to point out a golden eagle and a peregrine falcon. She did notice that as they rode his wide shoulders seemed to slowly relax.

The sun rose higher into the sky as they followed the narrow trail until it intersected with a well-traveled road from the south. They ventured onto the road and continued westerly. The salty air was familiar and welcoming, although it triggered a painful tightness in Freyja's chest. From the crest in the road, she witnessed the tranquil sight of two whaling boats heading out of the bay on a hunt. Freyja hadn't realized her horse had stopped until she saw Hugh watching her. She urged Saga ahead.

They rounded a curve in the road and Freyja gasped. She reined in her horse and marveled at the impressive, medieval castle. Perched high upon a hill not far from the beach, it stood as an ominous presence bearing down on anyone daring to approach it. The fortress rose high above the battlement wall and had the signs of multiple additions over the centuries since its construction.

"Come, lass, Corell Castle awaits," Hugh called over his shoulder. He glanced back at Freyja, then pulled Perseus to a halt. "If ye think this be daunting, wait till ye gaze upon the great hall and kirk."

Side by side they passed under the portcullis and entered the outer bailey. Her strong survival instinct commanded that she spin her horse around and flee.

Breathe, she told herself as they entered the inner bailey. Freyja noticed the blacksmith in the open-sided smithy, from the corner of her eye. The large man set his tools down, shielded his eyes and squinted when he strolled out into the sunlight. Several others ventured out to stand and gawk at them: or more precisely, at her. She should have never come with Hugh. The better plan would have been to flee, except, she knew Saga could never outrun Hugh's big palfrey, Perseus.

A stable boy appeared and took their horses. Hugh turned and motioned for Freyja to follow him. Freyja pulled her shoulders back, tilted her chin up, and rested her hand on the hilt of the backsword belted at her side. She matched her stride to Hugh's as they walked toward the keep. Scanning her surroundings, she imagined a place this massive would have a substantial dungeon, hopefully she would not be viewing it in person. As if Hugh sensed her apprehension, he glanced her way and with a solemn face, said, "All will be fine, love."

Freyja wondered what had been on his mind all morning, but she'd been too worried to ask him in case it had something to do with her performance of the night before.

In silence they marched up the wide stone steps, through the enormous, ancient wooden door. Once they entered the keep, they went down a long corridor before stopping at the arched entrance to a great hall. The stone walls were covered with colorful tapestries and several outstanding weapon displays. The stone floors were swept clean, and a delicious aroma filled the air. Low fires burned in the two gigantic fireplaces positioned at each end of the vast hall. Corell Castle was more than daunting; it was majestic. Despite its enormity, the warmth of the fires and the low hum of conversation made it unexpectantly homey, so different from her home. If she were not in danger, she might have imagined herself comfortable within its walls.

Two handsome dark-haired men were seated at the high table talking. She'd heard enough about the MacCormac clan, to guess the large ominous one of the two men, with the long black hair and thick beard was the infamous *Black Giant.* His power was evident by the way he arrogantly reclined with one leg hung over the side of his throne. His thick black brows were pulled tightly together while he seemed to study them when they entered. The other man who wore an amused expression, she presumed to be the younger, wily cousin, Malcolm. Three women were seated at the far end of the table. The one holding a baby on her lap, abruptly stood and handed the child over to the younger woman with straight black hair. The oldest woman nervously clasped her hands before her.

Hugh leaned forward and whispered next to her ear, "Of the two women approaching us, the older one is my Auntie, Lady Moira Sinclair and the other is, Lady Adriana MacCormac, the laird's wife." The two women grinned at Freyja and scurrying toward them. This was not good, surely, Lady Sinclair would recognize her and tell Lady Adriana who she is. Then the two dark-haired men stood. Laird MacCormac wore a fierce scowl as he descended the dais and strode forward. He was dressed in black trews, tall black boots that came to his knees, and a black leather jack. The only thing white was his starched shirt and cravat. His plaid hung over his broad shoulder and secured with an ancient looking bodkin. She glanced at his broadsword and wondered if he was ever without it.

As the women got closer, Lady Adriana stopped and Lady Sinclair took the last few steps closer, alone. Wringing her hands nervously she whispered, "Freyja?" Her face displayed both concern and happiness at seeing Freyja. She wrapped her arms around Freyja, pulling her into a tight hug. "Lass. 'Tis it truly ye? I never thought to see ye again." Hugh stood next to them, a confused expression on his face while he watched their exchange.

Laird MacCormac stopped beside his wife, leaned down and muttered in a loud enough voice that Freyja heard him say, "Here we go again. Even as a young lad, Hugh had the gift for rescuing all types of forsaken creatures. He saved many and returned them to the wild after hours of doctoring. I wonder where he found this wild looking person and what he plans to do with her."

By everyone else's nervous expression, Freyja hadn't been the only one who overheard his remark. She stiffened and glared at the chieftain and felt a little of her fear diminish.

Hugh introduced her to everyone. When he presented her as Freyja Rasmusdatter, the surname she had given him, his aunt stepped back and gave her a quizzical look. As Hugh finished the introductions, Freyja stayed silent and prayed the woman wouldn't give her secret away. As the chieftain's wife and hostess of the castle, Lady Adriana stepped forward. With a big grin, she looped her arm through Freyja's. "You come with me dear," she said. "We will get you in a hot bath, then some clean clothes, and a good meal." She ushered Freyja toward the steps and requested hot water to be brought up to the burgundy room and for someone to fetch Bethany right away. Then Freyja noticed the young dark-haired woman, holding a baby, who stood back a few steps. They made eye contact. One perfect black brow arched above the lass's keen eyes and Freyja knew, Sorcha Sinclair recognized her.

Cam turned and scowled at Hugh and Malcolm. "My office, noo." Hugh sighed at the authoritative tone in his cousin's voice. He watched Adriana lead Freyja up the stone steps. Then something caught his attention. Aunt Moira and Sorcha were standing off to the side with their heads close together, whispering as they also watched Adriana and Freyja ascend the steps. What where they up to? Mayhap he didn't want to really know. His auntie's only reason for traveling so far from Sinclair Castle was because she was cooking up some sort of mischief.

Malcolm punched Hugh's shoulder. "Ye coming, cousin?"

Hugh frowned at Malcolm. "Aye."

Hugh was about to take a step when he heard a soft voice. "If ye hae a moment, Cousin Hugh, I would like to speak to ye." Hugh glanced down and found Sorcha smiling up at him.

How had she crossed the distance between them so fast, he wondered. "I donae hae time, lass. 'Twill hae to wait."

With his teeth clenched tightly, Hugh glanced from Sorcha to Malcolm, then walked away from Sorcha. Malcolm chuckled and leaned close to Hugh as they followed Cam down the corridor. "So, where did ye come across this lass? Cleaned up, she just might be bonnie." Hugh ignored Malcolm's remark. He had no desire to reveal anything more than he had to, nor a moment before they were behind the thick door of Cam's office.

Malcolm stopped in front of Cam's door, raised one hand as he turned to face Hugh. "So, tell me, where did ye dig her up?" When Malcolm paused, Hugh knew the precise moment his cousin realized who the lass was. "No?" Malcolm's eyes grew large and round. He placed his hand on Hugh's shoulder he continued, "Tell me ye dinnae go back and dig up the dead lass?"

Hugh shrugged off his cousin's hand and walked into Cam's office, ignoring Malcolm's laughter. Mayhap he should have given more thought before bringing Freyja here. His cousin made no attempt to cover his amusement as he entered the office behind him.

Three glasses of brandy had been poured and placed across the front of the huge oak desk. Hugh reached for one and downed it in one gulp. Malcolm and Cam exchanged a look as they drank their brandy. When Malcolm grinned and refilled the glasses, Hugh wanted to punch his cousin in the face. What did he think was so funny anyway? Hugh downed a second glass.

Cam scowled and snatched the bottle of brandy away from Malcolm. "Pour his from the other bottle," he said. "Donae be wasting my good brandy on him. He's not tasting it anyways. Sit," Cam ordered. "We hae business to take care of." Hugh and Malcolm settled into the chairs before the desk. "Noo," Cam said, perching himself on the corner of his desk and glaring down at Hugh. "I think ye hae a few things to explain."

Hugh had not been looking forward to this conversation, but it was inevitable. He held out his empty glass, but Cam hesitated before refilling it. He drained the glass and sighed. "My conscience wouldnae let me leave the lass half buried in the woods. She deserved a proper burial."

Cam frowned. He glanced at Malcolm and then back to Hugh, and asked, "The lass that walked into the Great Hall with ye? Who buried her in the woods?"

"We found her a few days ago," Malcolm said, waving a hand at Cam. "On our way back from Edinburgh."

Cam's frown deepened. Scratching his beard Hugh continued, "When I found her still alive I dinnae know what to do with her. I couldnae bring her here in case she be a MacDonald. Besides, the castle was too far. She would hae surely died by the time we arrived, so I took her to the old hunting lodge by the loch. 'Twas easier to tend to her wounds there. She was safe and warm there until I knew if she was going to live or not."

He shared everything with his cousins, except for the part about taking her maidenhead the night before, and the fact that he'd planned to ask Cam for his permission to marry her.

Malcolm chuckled off and on while Hugh told his story. Cam sat quietly, appearing dumbstruck by the whole incident. After a long uncomfortable silence, Cam asked, "Hae ye thought aboot what ye plan to do with the lass?"

Hugh saw Malcolm's shoulders shake as he stifled his laughter and refilled his glass. "Based on his surly mood, I think he's already done what he wanted to do with the lass. Though he's not likely to confess any of the details to us." Hugh turned and scowled at Malcolm, which earned him an outright laugh.

"Weel," Cam said, standing and moving to the window. "Ye'll have plenty of time to think aboot what ye want while we're gone. I hae been called to a chieftain's meeting at Kirkbridge House, and ye both and a few troops are riding with me. Big Alec is getting the men and supplies together as we speak. I know not what's afoot, but ye can bet it has something to do with the loyalists' doings for the King. We must leave at once else we will be on the road all night and miss most of the meeting tomorrow morning. So be saying yer farewells quickly, then meet me in the outer bailey."

Hugh headed above stairs to find Freyja. He didn't want to leave her so soon after arriving, but she would be safe here, and Adriana, Bethany, and Aunt Moira would look after her. Freyja was smart and quick witted, he knew the women would become fast friends.

Nearing Freyja's door, he heard Freyja laughing. He knocked twice and Lady Adriana pulled the door open. Barefooted and dressed in only a shift, Freyja stepped around Lady Adriana toward him. Without a hint of shyness, she smiled as Hugh stood at the threshold and took her hands in his. "I hae but a moment."

"Why, what has happened?"

He saw a glimmer of panic in her eyes. He sighed and squeezed her hands. "I must leave right away with Laird MacCormac."

"How long will you be gone," she asked.

"I know not when we shall return. But, as long as ye stay here with Lady Adriana, Bethany, and my aunt ye will be safe." She nodded her head as he spoke. "They will take good care of ye."

"Yes, of course we will," Lady Adriana said, "I will personally watch over her."

Freyja smiled but feared it didn't hide her disappointment at Hugh leaving even though she wouldn't' be here when he returned. She had wanted to spend a little more time with him before she snuck away.

"I must go, lass." Hugh pulled her into his arms. His kiss was gentle. When he pulled back, Freyja reached out and placed her hand against his rough cheek. She wanted to gaze into those passionate, amber eyes one last time.

He kissed her again then turned and walked away.

Reluctant to face Lady Adriana after such a display of affection, Freyja turned around slowly. Lady Adriana's brows were raised, and Freyja felt the heat of a blush as it rose from her toes to the top of her head. Lady Adriana's smirk crept into a full grin. "It is good to see him so. Makes me happy Hugh has finally found someone he cares so much for."

"Aye, milady. I too, am grateful that he found me; otherwise, I would certainly be dead by now." Seeing Lady Adriana's shocked expression, and knowing where her thought must have taken her, Freyja quickly added, "Although he had found me beaten and abandoned in the woods, I assure you I belong to neither the MacDonald's nor the Campbell's. And I swear I do not wish any harm upon you and your clan."

Lady Adriana sighed, stepped forward, placed a comforting hand on Freyja's arm, and squeezed it gently. "Off course you don't, dear. However, if you feel a need to discuss anything, I am here for you. I would like for you to feel at home here."

Home. Freyja no longer had a place she could call home. But soon she would return to Dreki Craige Castle, with all its dragon statues and carvings and confront her brother. She wrapped her arms around herself. With Hugh and Laird MacCormac gone for a few days, her plans to leave would be much easier to achieve.

Freyja jumped when the door swung open and a petite woman with brown-hair and a big friendly grin swept into the chambers like a wild windstorm. She instructed the two strapping lads carrying a large tub to set it down. They were followed by several more servants carrying buckets of steaming water. Lady Adriana placed a blanket over Freyja's shoulders, turned her around, and led her away from curious eyes.

When they heard the door close, she turned Freyja back around. The woman who had arrived with the tub stood alone, her hands on her hips and a lopsided grin on her enthusiastic face. She inspected Freyja's tall womanly frame. "No wonder Hugh dinnae look twice at his cousin Sorcha. Ye are a bonnie lass."

"This is my lady's maid, Bethany," Lady Adriana said, interrupting Freyja's thoughts. "She will get you cleaned up and properly dressed."

The steaming water looked inviting, yet Freyja hesitated. What were they going to think when they saw her many scars? The recent scars were still raised and red. Even though the bruising on her sides, back, and legs were no longer greenish-purple, they were still quite noticeable. Knowing there was no way to hide herself from their eyes, Freyja raised her chin, dropped the blanket, and pulled the shift over her head and tossed it on the floor. As she stepped into the tub, from behind her she heard Bethany remark, "Jesus, Mary and Joseph."

Ignoring the woman's comment, she sank down into the deep tub and released a long sigh. She had never bathed in such a large tub before, and it felt heavenly. Picking up the cake of soap, Freyja started lathering up her hair. Unexpectedly, Bethany was taking the soap from her. "Let me do this for ye. Ye hae such beautiful hair. I hae never seen honey colored hair streaked with red and gold, 'tis lovely." Bethany scrubbed Freyja's head, then massaged her scalp. This was a new experience for Freyja, and she was loving it. She moaned and let the woman work her magic.

"'Tis been a long while since we had such an interesting woman as yerself show up at the castle. Take our own Lady Adriana here," Bethany said as she scrubbed Freyja's tender skin. "Two years ago, Laird MacCormac and his warriors had been attacked and The MacCormac was badly wounded. Lady Adriana appeared like the angel he called her and married him and looked after his wounds." Bethany shook the bar of soap as she spoke. "Our mistress here," she pointed at Lady Adriana. "She tended to him each day and night and forced him to swallow broth and water. She saved his life."

Freyja glanced over to where the young woman sat on the bed tying little blue bows along the bottom of a skirt. The woman smiled shyly. "Don't be thinking I am a saint, because I can assure you I am not," she said, smiling. "Someday, maybe I'll tell you the whole story."

"Pretty close to a saint if ye be asking me," Bethany said, kneeling at the end of the tub. She scrubbed Freyja's feet and legs. Then bluntly asked, "Are ye and Hugh lovers, then?"

"Bethany!" Lady Adriana scolded from where she was fussing over some garments. "You needn't ask such a question of the lass. It is none of our business."

Bethany huffed and shrugged. "Oh, the big dobber cannae hide something like this from me. 'Twas just I figured he'd been spending his time with the widow McEwen. But he kept returning for supplies... And I'm guessing the healing salve was for ye," she added, smiling at Freyja, and then winked. Lady Adriana hastily pulled a chair toward the end of the tub and sat down. The two women stared, anticipating a tantalizing tale.

Freyja wanted to slide down under the water and disappear. Lovers? "No. We are not lovers and I doubt we ever will be." She wished she knew how he did feel about their coupling. He only acknowledged what had happened the night before was when he kissed her good night.

When Freyja glanced up, doubtful expressions marred the two women's faces. Bethany sat back on her heels and placed her fists on her hips. "Weel, then I guess 'tis all right that Lady Moira brought Miss Sorcha Sinclair here to marry Hugh. If that meddling old woman gets her way it will happen right when he returns." Bethany raised a brow as if gauging Freyja's reaction.

Freyja could still feel the sensation of Hugh's lips on her breasts, and heat rose to her face. Not from the warm bath or the lingering memory, but from a burning ache deep in her core even though she tried to force it back down. She had figured her, and Hugh's time together would be short-lived, but how could she give him up to Sorcha Sinclair of all people.

Sinclair Castle had been several kilometers to the east of Dreki Craige Castle, and when they were young, Freyja and Sorcha had played together. It had been years since she had seen the girl, and she wasn't sure she would even recognize her. The announcement of Sorcha marrying Hugh surprised Freyja. As far as she knew, Sorcha and her own brother, Finlay, were still betrothed. And as the new laird, she was sure Finlay would want to marry as soon as he could. He was also not one to concede anything easily, especially the Sinclair name and power it would give him. Finlay would surely come looking for his betrothed.

What if he were already on his way here?

Ten

Freyja stood hidden from view in the corridor outside the Great Hall. She brushed a trembling hand over the intricately embroidered flowers on the white waistcoat she wore, wishing she was in the worn trews, boots, and waistcoat she'd arrived in. She had protested at the first sight of the light pink linen shift and overshirt, but Bethany had insisted the worn clothes she had found at the hunting lodge be taken away and burned, leaving her with only the feminine garb she now wore.

Bethany and Lady Adriana had fussed over Freyja, something she was not used to. First a bath, which she would have liked to lie back and relax in had she been alone in the room. Bethany placed Freyja before the fire to dry her hair, while she inspected and tended to her injuries. She then brushed out Freyja's long think hair and pinned it all up on top of her head, letting a couple strands fall free to curl around her neck. Growing up without a mother, Freyja couldn't remember anyone fussing over her like this before. Their bustling around kept the two women busy and allowed Freyja to forget her problems for a while. She actually enjoyed spending the day listening to their easy interactions and experiencing their caring attention, even if the final results of their efforts left her feeling self-conscience and vulnerable to scrutiny.

Drawing in an encouraging breath, Freyja entered the great hall for supper. A few people she hadn't met yet wandered about. She spotted Lady Adriana across the room and with a sigh of relief, headed toward her. Lady Adriana held her son, a little dark-haired boy about two years old. As she approached Lady Adriana, the little boy's eyes widened, and he smiled and reached both arms out to her. "I think he likes you, Freyja," Lady Adriana said. "Would you care to hold him?"

"Oh, yes," Freyja replied. "but I'm not practiced at holding little ones."

Lady Adriana laughed. "He takes after his father," she said, handing the lad to Freyja. "He's tough. Although, since he's learned to walk, he will take off running if you set him down and let go of him."

Freyja held the boy on her hip and giggled, "You need to inform your mother that boys dash about like newborn colts all the time." Freyja lovingly fondled the lad's tight black curls.

Robbie's small chubby hand reached out to grab one of the earbobs fastened to Freyja's earlobe. "Oh, don't you dare you little thief," his mother said, pulling his arm away.

Robbie's hands flapped about as if shewing away a swarm of bees, then let out a high-pitched yell. Freyja quickly captured both of the boy's hands and, in a calm but stern voice, said, "Robbie, there will be no screeching in the hall. Do you understand?"

The boy quieted down and gaped at her, and Freyja released his hand. "There now," she said with a smile, "that's a good boy." Robbie laid is head on Freyja's chest, and she lowered herself onto a chair and gently rubbed the boy's back. When she glanced up, everyone was watching her.

"Oh, that was impressive," Lady Adriana said, staring at her. "I think I had better keep you here to help me with him. Ever since he has learned to walk, he yells like a banshee if he doesn't get his own way, or if you try to restrain him."

Freyja grinned. "Hardheaded men, even little men," she kissed the top of his head. "Need to be handled with a firm hand."

"'Tis like his father he is," said a short round woman with a fake stern expression, appeared before them in her stained and faded apron. She stepped forward and curtsied. "Me names Maddy, mistress. Proud I am to meet ye."

"Thank you, Maddy." Freyja recalled the fondness within Hugh's voice when he'd spoke of this woman. "It is very nice to meet the woman whom Hugh holds so dearly in his heart. He speaks very kindly of you, Maddy."

The stout little woman blushed, then bobbed her head and said, "Let me take the wee tyrant to the kitchen." She reached out and Freyja handed the lad over to the cook. "I am sure I can find a tart or a chicken leg to keep him busy while ye eat yer supper."

"Thank you, Maddy," Lady Adriana said, patting her son's back.

Lady Adriana turned to Freyja. "Let me introduce you to everyone before dinner. It seems you already know my husband's aunt, Lady Moira Sinclair." Freyja curtsied and nodded her head. Lady Moira smiled. She had obviously refrained from saying anything about Freyja's true name to Lady Adriana, but Freyja could see the questioning look in the older woman's eyes.

She was introduced to Father Fitzgerald and the steward, Mr. Pembroke. Bethany, who Freyja promptly learned upheld not only the position of lady's maid to Lady Adriana, but also close friend and confidant, stood off to the side speaking to an enormous man, who was even bigger than laird MacCormac. The man had reddish-orange hair and kind blue eyes. "That gigantic man is Bethany's husband, Big Alec," Lady Adriana whispered as she pulled Freyja toward the end of the table. "And this lovely little thing is Miss Sorcha Sinclair. Miss Sorcha, may I present Freyja Rasmusdatter."

Sorcha nodded. "'Tis nice to make yer acquaintance." Freyja bobbed a slight curtsy and replied softly, "And yours."

Sorcha may not have informed anyone of Freyja's true identity. Nevertheless, she kept a close eye on everything Freyja did and listened intently to her conversations. It was obvious Sorcha had recognized her, and she feared the girl would inform the MacCormac of the charges against her. If that happened, she could be thrown into the dungeon and held for an actual trial.

Across the field from Kirkbridge House, Hugh walked along the riverbank, gathering armfuls of sticks and branches for their campfire. It had been dark and quiet when they arrived late the night before. Now, hundreds of tents lined the riverbank, woods, and were scattered throughout the open field.

When he had turned and glanced up at Freyja's window, he had hoped to catch a glimpse of her before he rode out. But it hadn't been Freyja's face which stared back at him but his cousin Sorcha's. He wondered why she had been up so early and watching them leave. Then his mind jumped to the image of Freyja and how she pretended to be an experienced lover kept haunting him. Certainly, she knew he would discover that she was a virgin. To what purpose would she act so? If she meant to secure his protection, there was no reason for her to sacrifice her virginity, she had only to ask. However, up until then she seemed more than adequate to take care of herself. He rubbed his palm over the lingering lump on the back of his head from when she hit him over the head and attempted to steal his horse. Evidently, she had planned to set out on her own without any help from anyone, but where had she planned to go? Perplexed, he shook his head. And what could have possessed her to come to him in only her shift?

Hugh returned to his camp, he built a small fire and set a pot of peeled apples on to boil, then sat back on a stump. Had her intent all along been to seduce him, in hopes of securing his protection, then why wouldn't she reveal the whole truth to him?

"Noo that's an expression I hae never seen on his face before," Malcolm said as he and Cam approached Hugh. "After riding for hours without a word last night, are ye ready to tell us what's got ye so tangled up inside?"

"Leave him be, Malcolm," Cam said, looking into the pot boiling on the fire. "Apple cider? Do ye hae bread to spread the apple mash on?"

Hugh had a pouch of floured buns which Maddy had given to him. He picked up the pouch that he'd been hiding for himself and tossed it at Cam, ignoring Malcolm's prying questions. His *insides* were none of his cousin's concern. He longed to be back at the castle with Freyja, yet he also knew he needed time away from her to think about her actions and sort his feelings. She was the most puzzling woman he had ever met.

"There's that look again," Malcomb said. He shook his head and dipped his cup into the pot. "Och, 'tis hot." They drank their cider and ate their floured rolls dripping with the sweet, hot, apple mash in silence.

Moments later, Cam motioned for a dozen MacCormac men to follow them to Kirkbridge House. Hugh stood and took his rightful place on Cam's right side. They entered the large stone house and strode down the corridor toward the hum of voices. As they entered the hall, Hugh glanced over to a table where a group of soldiers sat. Their statements were loud and crude. He counted sixteen men, and he recognized their plaids and arms as the same sixteen men he saw in the hunting party.

They greeted and shook hands with several of the clan chiefs before the meeting started. Each clan chief was given an opportunity to stand and voice their opinion on the recent massacre of the Glencoe MacDonalds. Frustrated, many shouted out their concerns.

"Soldiers and loyalists still hunt for those who escaped into the hills."

"Even though we signed the Royal Proclamation, what reassurance do we hae against our families being murdered in their sleep?"

"What 'tis gonna happen next?"

"King William has left Britain, leaving Queen Mary to rule in his stead."

"Aye, but William has a long reach."

"King William's message is quite clear. Ye either submit to his rule or be destroyed."

"Aye." Several other men called out in both anger and panic.

The MacCormac men remained silent. Their chief stood with his arms crossed over his broad chest, his brows pulled down in a fierce frown. The MacCormic's had deep alliances with many of the clan chiefs gathered there this day. Hugh knew none of those lairds would attempt any kind of action without the Black Giant's approval.

A young man no more than ten and five dressed for court and two rough-looking men entered the hall. They were followed closely by the sixteen men Hugh noticed seated at the table when they entered. Hugh overheard someone off to his right remark that the lad dressed in a black velvet justaucorps, intricately embroidered in gold, light blue, and rose was Laird Findlay Weir, the new chieftain of Dreki Craige Castle.

With the haughtiness of a seasoned Laird, Weir raised his hands commanding everyone's attention and spoke loudly. "'Tis evident to me that the clans band together and lay siege to King William and all Williamites."

Although his request was met with a mixture of murmurs and grumbles from the group, the young popinjay strutted about the great hall of Kirkbridge House in his gold brocade silk vest and knee-length breeches. His cravat and cuffs were made of white lace, and he wore white hose and black gold-buckled shoes. He carried a tricorne hat adorned with ostrich feathers under one arm, which Hugh imagined was so he would not disturb his long blonde wig. He persisted that since King William had left to fight elsewhere, this was the perfect time to strike.

Rumors of deceit and murder relating to the death of Weir's brother and previous chieftain, Laird Andrew Weir, quickly circulated throughout the assembly. Hugh overheard two MacPherson lads who stood close by grumbling about the tale. "I heard the eldest brother, Laird Andrew Weir, was murdered on his deathbed by his younger sister in a plot to take over the clan. The lass was charged and found guilty of murder. 'Tis said the new young laird of Dreki Craige Castle," he nodded his head toward Weir, "banished her from the Weir clan and forbad her to ever return."

"'Tis said," the other man replied, "The lass's honey coloured hair 'tis streaked with fire and she has the same blueish-green eyes of the new laird." He chuckled and scratched his bark beard. "I hae also heard, 'tis something to watch her handle a sword, knife, or bow."

Hugh staggered back a step, pleased to find a solid wall behind him and prayed he would not fall to the floor.

Did I hear correctly? They must be mistaken. Could it be Freyja, my Freyja?

The pieces all started to fit together: The silky hair that glowed when she neared the fire, the haunting blueish-green eyes, but mostly her skill with a weapon. Never before had he met a woman, much less a laird's daughter, who had trained to become a warrior. Hugh rubbed his aching forehead.

Somewhere in the back of his mind a memory crept forward. A story told by his Aunt Moira, about the daughter of Laird Lochlan Weir of Dreki Craige Castle on the northern coast. A tale stating that after her mother had died, the young lass strived to be accepted by her father and brothers. How the lass took to following her older brothers around, and while learning to fight with a sword and dirk, she grew tall and strong. A lass with piercing eyes the color of the sea and honey colored hair streaked with red and gold and glowed like fire in the sun.

Hugh's stomach twisted in knots. He wiped his damp palm on his plaid. He felt a strong urge to confront the young laird and inquire about his sister. He wanted to know if she had received a fair trial, who had beaten her and then left her alone in the woods, to die in a shallow grave? His fingers slipped around the handle of his sword. He had a feeling he already knew the answers, and he didn't like it.

Hugh heard Cam swear under his breath as he and Malcolm drew in close to him on either side. Hugh let his cousins escort him from the hall. His thoughts lingered on the woman who had changed his well-ordered life completely. No woman had ever stirred such powerful feelings in him before. He came to the realization that if the lass really did kill her oldest brother, she must have had a good reason. Since Weir knew she still lived and had men searching for her, she would need his protection now, even more.

Freyja braided her hair, adjusted her shirt, then pulled on the sleeveless, brown, leather jack and laced up the front. Bethany had come earlier to her room with an armful of some wardrobe items she'd acquired from the household lads. The woman also stated that she was working on a lovely mossy-green gown for her. Freyja appreciated the attention Lady Adriana and Bethany were giving her, but she needed to concentrate on her plan to leave while Hugh and Laird MacCormac were gone. Dressed in clean trews, knee high brown boots, and some lad's shirt and buttery soft leather jack, she fastened her sword belt around her waist. Now that she had replacement clothes for the dirty, old worn ones she'd arrived in, she needed to find out which of the paddocks Saga was being kept in. By the afternoon she would be ready to make her escape from Corell Castle.

Freyja trekked across the inner bailey toward the stables. Noticing the circular training ring, out of habit, she crawled through the rails and tested the loose deep sand beneath her feet.

"'Tis it exercise or instruction yer looking for, lass?" A deep good-humored voice asked from behind her.

Freyja spun around and found the giant guard, Big Alec crawling through the rail. He raised one bushy reddish-orange brow, and his dark blue eyes twinkled with a hint of boyish mischief as he watched her closely. The big man grinned and slowly slid his sword from its scabbard. Between his sheer size and the length of his broadsword, he became even more of an opposing figure. "Ye hae no answered me, lass."

Taking a step back, Freyja pulled her sword and replied, "Mayhap a little of each." The big warrior stepped to his right. She took a step to her right. If he wanted her dead, the deed would have already been done. He was merely testing her. Wondering if she could hold her own against him. Two men rushed toward them each holding a wooden targe. Alec lowered his sword arm, nodded once, and the soldiers quickly crawled through the rails. The soldier who came to Freyja held the shield steady and she slipped her arm through the leather straps. Before he left the ring, he struck the wooden shield twice with his fist, nodded his head wishing her a good and fair match. Freyja wrapped her fingers around the leather strap and raised it up to shoulder height. Questioning her sanity for agreeing to the big warrior's challenge she prayed he would not cleave her in two.

With his own shield secured to his arm, Alec took the first step, and the dance began. Freyja studied the man, waiting for him to make a move. But when he didn't advance, she drew in a deep breath and moved forward. She had only taken two steps when he said, "Donae draw a breath afore ye attack someone who is so close to ye. It gives yer intentions away. Watch yer opponent closely. Watch for him to make a mistake, then attack. Ye want yer strike to be a surprise."

As he took another step, Freyja advanced and swung her sword, hitting his targe when he blocked her strike. "Aye, lass. Yer a quick learner." He nodded his head and said, "Let us be on with this."

They continued, each striking the others' sword and shield. Soon a group of men had gathered around the training ring and were cheering and clapping. His strikes were hard, and her body still ached where she'd taken the worst of the beating, and she felt the pain all the way up her arm and through her body. The ground was uneven and soft in some areas and Freyja struggled to keep her footing. Soon she stood panting, dripping with sweat. Big Alec crawled out of the ring and Freyja exhaled; glad his training was over. But then the huge warrior grabbed a lad and tossed the boy over the rail into the ring. He stood outside the ring, laughing and shouting words of encouragement to the young lad. Each time a lad fell and crawled out of the ring, Big Alec tossed in another. Freyja had never fought in a battle, and she knew these soldiers were holding back, but she remembered her training and fought back hard with great determination. She needed them all to know that if the need ever came, she would fight beside them as a warrior, not a simpering female.

The crowd of men along the rail had grown. Freyja wiped the back of her arm across her damp brow. Another lad entered the training ring. He appeared older than the others. He flipped his sword over the back of his hand then whipped it through the air, first on one side of his body, then the other. There was a menacing glint in his eyes that warned her to be wary of this soldier.

He circled around her, casting glances to the men outside of the ring. Then he lunged forward with his sword raised. Freyja maintained her position, blocking his attack with her shield. She remained still, making only minor adjustments as he continued to move around her. Sparring with four lads before him, left her tired and her muscles ached. Her strategy was to conserve energy, while he expended his through displays of swordsmanship. Impatient, he snarled and advanced. Freyja was ready for him and whirled to the side, bringing her sword down, tapping the flat surface against his backside. He swiped wildly, forcing her back. She raised her targe and warded off another strike. They fought for several more moments until a blow knocked her to the ground. He raised his sword poised to strike but Freyja rolled, swiped her leg out and knocked the man to the ground. Jumping to her feet, she stepped on his blade and pointed her sword at his throat. She was no longer the pupil; she'd become the teacher.

Outside of the ring the soldiers roared and clapped at her accomplishment. Freyja lowered her sword arm to her side then reached out her hand to help the man up. She flinched with pain as his weight strained the muscles in her shoulder and aggravated the pain along her ribs.

"She's a good match for Hugh, wouldn't you agree?" Freyja overheard Adriana, standing by the rail say to Big Alec. "Aye, lass she is."

Freyja gingerly crawled through the rails to were Lady Adriana stood holding Robbie in her arms. Turning to Big Alec, Freyja said, "I have been schooled. Your intention was clear."

Big Alec laughed then clapped her on the shoulder and said, "Ye hae been trained weel afore ye arrived here. Ye did yerself proud, lass." Surprised at the man's kind and reassuring praise, Freyja nodded her thanks and honored him with a deep bow, hoping he hadn't noticed she still suffered from her injuries.

Robbie reached out both arms to Freyja. Smiling she took the boy from his mother. "Hea ye been a good boy today?" She asked him with a Scottish accent. Robbie responded with a loud, "Baa," like a baby lamb.

"He has been bothering me all morning to bring him down to the barns to see the newborn lambs," Adriana said.

"Oh, that sounds like a lovely outing, doesn't it, Robbie?"

Freyja asked, poking her finger against the boy's tummy. He let out another loud lamb sound, and everyone laughed.

Freyja followed Lady Adriana out of the inner bailey toward a row of small buildings along the battlement wall. Lady Adriana turned to Freyja. "Who trained you to fight like that?" Freyja shrugged, avoiding the question. Wanting to get down, Robbie wiggled in Freyja's arms. "You don't have to carry him," his mother said. "He thinks he no longer needs to be held and carried everywhere." Freyja set the boy down and he quickly toddled off. "Don't go too far, Robbie," his mother yelled. Then she turned and stared at Freyja.

Freyja didn't want to lie to her ladyship, yet she couldn't reveal very much about her past to her either. "Where I once lived, there was an old warrior who felt I needed to learn to defend myself."

"So, you didn't have any parents or someone to protect you?"

"No," Freyja answered. "I enjoyed the training." She glanced ahead just as Robbie disappeared around the back of a building. Freyja bolted after the boy. As she drew closer, she heard the boy bark like a dog. Then she heard a dog growl. Terrified at what she might find, Freyja pulled her knife from her boot and rounded the side of the building. There stood *not* a large dog but a hungry wolf that had come to feast on a pile of birthing remains. She heard Lady Adriana gasp behind her. The wolf's lips curled up, and he bared its teeth, its eyes trained on Robbie. Keeping her eyes on the animal, Freyja stepped in front of the lad and said, "Take Robbie back to the castle." When she didn't hear any movement behind her Freyja commanded, "Now."

Lady Adriana called out, "Robbie, come to me."

Out of the corner of her eye, Freyja saw Robbie's chubby little arms waving in the air, then Lady Adriana scooped up her son and backed away. The large wolf lowered its head watching Freyja and continued to growl. With her free hand, Freyja slowly slid her sword out of its sheath. "Go on with ye now," she yelled hoping to scare the wolf off. Except the wolf wasn't interested in leaving his newly found feast. She stomped toward him, waved her arms, and yelled again, but he still wouldn't turn and run off.

The child was now safe with his mother, and she doubted the wolf would leave the treasure he'd found. Freyja started to back away. Best to let him eat in peace. As she turned to walk away, the wolf charged toward her, knocking her off her feet. Freyja rolled onto her side, raised her sword just as the animal sprang forward. Her blade sunk into the wolf and its lifeless body landed next to her on the ground. Freyja jumped to her feet, her heart slamming against her chest as she stared down at the animal. She was elated that she'd been able to save the lad yet also saddened for the animal's unavoidable demise.

After a moment she turned to find Lady Adriana clutching Robbie to her breasts and several guards standing at the edge of the building watching her. Big Alec stood only a couple of feet behind her, his sword drawn, ready to take over if the need arose. Then Freyja noticed Sorcha. The girl stood off to the side, her arms crossed over her chest. She glared at Freyja, shook her head disapprovingly, then turned and walked away.

Eleven

Laird Cameron ordered their camps torn down before dawn. Tents and cooking supplies were collected and placed in the supply wagon. Hugh drew his plaid over his head to keep the rain from streaming down the back of his neck. Once his bedroll was fastened onto his horse he mounted and fell into line next to Cam. His mind rambled over the unbelievable and shocking details he had learned at the chieftain's meeting. How was he to accept that his beautiful Freyja was in fact Freyja Weir of Clachan Craige, a laird's daughter.

On the heels of Laird Finlay's performance, Hugh was forced to acknowledge the resemblance between Freyja and the young laird. He wrestled all night with the information and was still leery to reveal the news to his cousins this morning. How was he expected to explain that Freyja was in fact the daughter of the great Laird Lockton Weir and sister to the new pompous young laird. But most of all, what was Cam going to do when he learned that she'd been found guilty of murdering her oldest brother, Laird Andrew.

Hugh rubbed his temple, troubled about what happened between he and Freyja. How was he expected to conduct yourself around her after taking her virginity and then to find out she was the daughter of a Laird?

"'Tis marvelous to be out in the fresh air, Malcolm said, "and away from a damp tent and a room full of sweaty, unwashed men." Malcolm paused and hesitantly added, "I learned some information that will be of great interest to ye, Hugh."

Hugh cringed. Had his cousins overheard the same rumors about Freyja that he had?

"I couldn't help but overhear a group of men state that little Miss Sorcha Sinclair is betrothed to the new chieftain of the Weir Clan, Laird Finlay."

Betrothed to Laird Weir? Hugh wasn't interested in marrying Sorcha, and he couldn't imagine the timid little Sorcha married to the pompous arse.

Malcolm cleared his throat and said, "If Auntie Moira gets her way, ye might have to fight Weir for Miss Sorcha's hand, cousin."

Hugh pushed the plaid off his head, leaned forward and looked around Cam to glare menacingly at Malcolm.

"I wonder if our sweet Auntie was even aware of the betrothal before they arrived at Corell Castle?"

Hugh snarled at Malcolm. "If I am forced to fight Weir, I assure ye it willnae be over Sorcha Sinclair." He'd pass this information on to his auntie as soon as he returned and arrange for his aunt and her subordinate to be escorted back to Sinclair Castle.

"It seems Laird Weir has misplaced his bride-to-be somehow," Malcolm said, playfully. "He has men combing the countryside looking for the lass."

Hugh gave his cousins a sharp glance and said, "That must be the hunting party I saw the other day on MacCormac land. They must have been looking for Sorcha."

If this were true, and Wier was at all responsible for Freyja's beating, he must believe she died in the woods that night from her injuries. What would happen if they came back searching for Sorcha and learned Freyja was still alive?

Staring straight ahead, Cam stated, "I too gained some interesting information while we were there. 'Tis rumored Finlay Weir recently became the new laird as the result of the death of his brother."

Malcolm added, "I heard the former laird was murdered."

Hugh grew uncomfortable, guilt-stricken over information he didn't want to reveal, yet he knew it would be easier to discuss before they reached the castle. "Aye, and what is more troublesome, I heard Laird Andrew was murdered by his sister." He sighed. "Miss Freyja Weir."

"We also heard this allegation," Cam said. "Do ye feel ye know the lass weel enough to judge if she is capable of committing murder?"

He shrugged his shoulders and said, "The lass does have a fierce temper. Once we hear her explanation, I'm sure it will prove her innocent of any wrongdoing. But innocent or guilty, I plan to marry the lass."

Malcolm and Cam reined in their mounts and stopped.

"Marry!" Cam said with a confused expression on his face. "Were ye gonna discuss this with me first?"

Malcolm shook his head and chuckled, "I wonder how Auntie Moira and Sorcha are going to react to this news?" More serious, he added, "And the fact that Weir has sent out search parties to locate his runaway betrothed."

"I donae care. Aunt Moira never informed me of any arrangements with Uncle Robert aboot me marrying Sorcha. Marrying Miss Freyja is what I wish to do." When Cam and Malcolm glanced at each other curiously, Hugh turned to Cam and added, "Once this cataclysm is cleared up, my plan is to speak with ye aboot restoring the old hunting lodge for me home."

"Is Miss Freyja aware of yer intentions?" Cam asked while

their small troop and supply wagon trekked along the road toward Corell Castle.

"I would think 'twould be apparent to her." At their inquisitive expressions, Hugh hesitated then added, "I took her maidenhead." He glanced away and stared off across the field. He hadn't planned on sharing that bit of information with his cousins. After a moment, he turned back. "Besides, she has no family who wants her. She needs protection from her brother." Or so he thought before the new information came to light about her possibly being a murderer.

"I wonder, with all this talk of lasses and marriage," Cam said with a teasing note in his voice. "Do ye think since Auntie Moira is set on Hugh being married, she has taken advantage of the time we've been away to educate *both* of Hugh's young lasses in the art of lovemaking, like she did me sweet Adriana afore we married?"

Hugh reined in his horse and stopped. His auntie wouldn't actually instruct Freyja and Sorcha as she had with Adriana, would she? His two cousins glanced over their shoulders at Hugh and laughed at the predicament he was quickly finding himself in.

Even though Hugh tried to appear amused at his cousin's jesting, his thoughts were all jumbled up. Had Freyja truly killed her brother, or had she been unjustly accused? Was her failure to divulge her story to him an admission of her guilt? If she were truly responsible for her brother's death, that would surely mean the loss of their future and her demise. Either way, someone had left her for dead once, there would be no stopping them if they were given another chance.

~

Freyja watched Lady Adriana stroll across the lady's parlor toward her. Today her ladyship's hair had been pulled back and held in place by several tiny flower-shaped pearl pins, which made it easy for Freyja to view the long scar on the right side of her face that ran from her hairline to her chin. The petite woman flopped into a chair and released a heavy sigh. "I swear at times Robbie can be as much of a handful as his father."

Freyja smiled when the exhausted mother relaxed back in the chair and closed her eyes. Just above a whisper, she said, "I miss my sister Lynette every time she returns home after one of her lengthy visits here." She opened her eyes, turned toward Freyja, adding, "She and my father are all the family I have. Though my father has learned, with good reason, to keep a great distance between himself and my husband."

Freyja turned and glanced at the large wooden doors fearing Laird MacCormac's return. A giant of a man, he stood a couple of inches taller than Hugh, but where Hugh had striking amber eyes and hair, The MacCormac's long hair, beard, and mustache were black. His eyes were also dark and quite menacing as if he could see right into one's soul. The man's arms and legs were thick and muscular, his chest broad and deep, which she figured caused the low rumbling, foreboding, sound that emerged when he spoke.

Freyja noted the differences between the laird and his wife as Lady Adriana's gentle voice interrupted her thoughts. "It is too bad you hadn't any siblings. A sister of your own at least. Even though I had only one sister, I felt lucky to have her." She appeared thoughtful for a moment then chuckled. "Dealing with all the men around here makes up for not growing up with brothers of my own though."

Freyja glanced down at her hands clasped on her lap. She had no idea what Hugh had told his family about her, but she liked Lady Adriana. She was easy to talk to. "Well, I once had two brothers," Freyja replied. "I used to chase them all over the estate. They said because I was a girl I couldn't do the things boys could do. I think I was ten and two when they informed me that girls were only good for making babies, cooking and cleaning, and doing needlework."

Lady Adriana glanced over to Freyja and said, "That was a terrible thing for them to say to you."

"I guess I was bothersome." Freyja shrugged. "My mother died when I was ten. I miss the life we had before my mother passed. That's when everything changed."

"I was also ten when my mother died," Lady Adriana said, reaching over and placing her hand on Freyja's. Freyja cleared her throat and continued. "My father became too busy with his chieftain duties to have much time for me. I must have been lonely, so I took to dressing like my brothers, following them everywhere, and copying everything they did." She offered a slight grin and added, "I learned to fight with a sword, wrestle, and anything else they did."

Lady Adriana smiled appreciatively. "Yes, I would say you are quite skillful with your sword, which I very much appreciate."

Freyja had come to know how to hunt, fish, climb trees, and stand guard, but most importantly, she had learned to take care of herself. But in doing all those things, she hadn't realized that her brothers grew to resent her. They teased her, kept secrets from her, and even threw rocks at her, so that she would leave them alone. Now she understood just how much they truly disliked her, especially Finlay. The thought of Finlay brought to mind her plan to leave while Hugh was away. However, she hadn't learned which pasture Saga was kept in.

After a few moments, Freyja stood and excused herself. She hurried down the corridor heading for her bedchamber. She needed to change into her trews and boots, gather her pack then locate Saga. As she reached the steps she heard a soft voice behind her calling her name. Freyja whirled around. Sorcha strolled toward her, the girl's controlled demeaner revealing nothing of her purpose as she approached. Freyja had no idea if Sorcha was aware of what happened at Dreki Craige Castle. She still needed to thank the girl for not revealing who she really was. There was a chance that the news of her brother's death hadn't reached Sinclair Castle before Sorcha and Lady Moira left on their journey south. However, that didn't explain her reason for not pointing out Freyja's true identity.

"Sorcha," Freyja smiled, "I wanted to thank you for not exposing me in front of everyone earlier."

The lass smiled slightly and said, "I will make ye a promise not to inform her ladyship that ye lied about yer name and the fact that ye murdered yer brother Andrew—if ye promise to leave afore Hugh and Laird Cameron return."

The girl's threat surprised Freyja. She had always though Sorcha timid and introverted, certainly not capable of being intimidating. "Sorcha, you must believe me, I did not kill Andrew."

Sorcha glanced around, pinned Freyja with her bold stare and whispered, "That is none of my concern. But ye must understand, there is no way I am going to marry Finlay and right noo, ye are the only thing that stands between me and Hugh."

"I understand Lady Sinclair brought you here to marry Hugh, Sorcha, but know that if Finlay hasn't agreed to end your betrothal, he will surely come searching for you. Marrying Hugh would start a feud between Finlay and the MacCormacs."

Sorcha turned away from Freyja and rubbed her hands up and down her arms but showed no emotion.

"Sorcha," Freyja pleaded, "Don't you care if hundreds of men, friends and family members are killed?"

"I donae care."

"What does your father say about this? Surely he would get involved in the fighting."

The girl spun back around to face her. "I donae care what my father thinks either. But mark my words, Freyja. If yer here in the morning I will go straight to Lady Adriana and tell her everything."

Freyja watched Sorcha turn and stomp away. Though she

had planned to leave Corell Castle as soon as she could, she did not wish for there to be bloodshed between the two clans. She had to stop Finlay before he started to search for Sorcha.

Twelve

Horns announced the return of Laird MacCormac and his warriors as they came within view of Correll Castle. Moments later the small troop and one supply wagon ambled under the portcullis into the outer bailey, the only sounds from the weary group were of crunching gravel under the horse's hoofs and wagon wheels, and the squeaking of harness leather. It had been a somber journey, during which a mixture of emotions assaulted Hugh's thoughts like giant waves crashing against a rocky shoreline, making him have reservations about his future.

Eager to seek out Freyja, Hugh pushed passed Cam and Malcolm and entered the Great Hall first. He stopped. His breath came hard and quick as he scanned the large chambers searching for the lass, praying she hadn't left. After a moment, he spotted her. All of a sudden, Hugh realized he didn't know what he had been expecting to find. It pleased him to see Freyja stayed true to herself and was dressed in brown trews, brown leather knee boots, a white shirt, and a brown leather jack. Seeing her sitting cross-legged on the floor playing wooden farm animals with Robbie, she looked more like a child herself and not someone who could possibly commit murder to someone who was already on their deathbed.

Lady Adriana hurried toward Cam. Laying her hand on his sleeve Hugh heard her say, "Milord, our guest Freyja slayed a wolf which was about to attack Robbie."

He heard his cousin mumble a reply to his wife concerning Freyja and her connection to her brother's death. Hugh turned and leered at Cam.

A single black brow rose in response to Hugh's expression. Then Cam glanced down at his wife and said, "Bring the lass to my office." As she scurried away Cam addressed Hugh. "Follow me." He then turned to Malcolm and commanded him to stand guard at the door.

Freyja whipped her single braid over her shoulder and wiped her damp palms on her trews as she paused in the corridor before Laird MacCormac's office. Why hadn't she heeded Sorcha's warning and left during the night instead of missing Hugh and falling asleep with thought of how wonderful it had been to fall asleep in his arms after they made love. Now she wondered what waited for her on the other side of the door. Lady Adriana offered a reassuring smile and knocked twice on the large wooden door. Freyja feared she was moments away from either her freedom or her demise.

The door swung open. Freyja drew in a raged breath. Then Lady Adriana's hand encouragingly gripped her elbow and guided her into the chamber. Lady Adriana let go of her arm and crossed to stand next to her husband, her head barely reached his shoulder.

"Freyja Weir of Clachan Greige," Cam said, drawing her attention to him. "I am told we owe ye our gratitude for saving our son from a dangerous wolf." Freyja nodded her head; her stomach had twisted into knots when he'd addressed her by her customary title. She had feared they would learn something about her on their travels, and it seemed her fears were warranted. Hugh came and stood next to her; she couldn't read his face by his blank expression.

"We shall talk again after ye, and Hugh are finished. It would seem ye hae much to discuss." He gestured to a chair by his desk. "Please sit."

Lady Adriana smiled and gave Freyja's arm a quick squeeze as she and her husband walked out and closed the door behind them.

Freyja wondered what the men had been told and by whom. Hugh sat on the edge of his chair as if he was ready to pounce on her at any second.

He stared at her for a moment. His breath appeared ragged, and his mouth was tight and straight. "Ye need to know lass that we met the new laird of Dreki Craige Castle at Kirkbridge." His voice was stern as he studied her closely. "He's verra young and verra eager for recognition and riches. He spined a good yarn, and it seems he would do and say anything if it were to his benefit." He paused for a moment then added, "'Twould seem these are strong family traits, wouldn't ye say?"

Freyja surged to her feet and glared down at him. Teeth clenched, heart pounding, her nails bit into the palms of her hands, she stated, "Don't you dare accuse me of something you know nothing about."

Hugh stood and headed for the door. "I willnae be yelled at by the woman who humiliated me afore my clansmen." Turning back to face her, he added, "I should have been told this news from ye. I want nothing from ye except for the truth." To show his authority, he folded his muscular arms across his broad chest. "I want to know everything that happened to ye until the moment I dug yer half-frozen body out of a grave in the woods."

Freyja drew in a deep breath, held it for a moment then released it slowly. The last thing she wanted to do was relive that horrible day again, but she knew the time had come to tell him everything.

As if defeated, Freyja sank down into the chair, her shoulders rounded, and she stared at her folded hands on her lap. When she spoke, her voice was so soft that Hugh had to strain to hear her.

"My father had been sick," she started slowly. "He suffered with a terrible cough and pains in his head for a long time. He could no longer think or speak clearly."

Hugh settled back onto his chair. He could see this was painful for her to talk about, and he wanted to hold her in his arms and comfort her. He forced himself to sit quietly and listen. Discern if she was telling him the truth or just more lies.

"I was ten and seven when he died. My oldest brother, Andrew, became Laird and Chieftain of Clan Weir. Shortly after, he also became ill and took to his bed."

Hugh remembered his auntie expressing her concern over the passing of the old laird of Dreki Craige Castle.

She shook her head from side to side as she continued. "My other brother, Finlay, easily took the position of chieftain when Andrew could no longer get out of bed. When Andrew started to show signs of improvement within the past few months," she glanced up, her eyes brimming with tears, "I truly believed he was going to recover." She swallowed hard. "Like every other night since he took to his bed I was there in his chambers. He enjoyed having me read to him. Sometimes I rubbed healing oils into his skin hoping it would relieve his cough and ease his breathing. I also helped the maids change his night shirts and bedding. This particular night I was in Andrew's chambers behind the privacy screen checking the chamber pot, when I heard his chamber door scrape across the stone floor, and then footsteps in the room. I stayed quiet as no one had announced their arrival. Eventually, I peered around the screen, I saw Finlay and his two bloody goons, Torcall and Dunn who never leave his side, cross to the bed. Finlay instructed them to stand on either side of the bed and hold Andrew still." Her hands trembled when she paused for a moment. "Finlay placed a pillow over Andrew's face and pressed it down," she whispered.

Closing her eyes, she rubbed her hand along her cheek then around the back of her neck. After a moment she resumed her tale. "I ran out from behind the screen and tried to stop them. I flew at Finlay, but he elbowed me away and held the pillow down even tighter. He growled at Torcall to silence me. Torcall grabbed for me. I swung my fist at him and caught him along side of his face. He swore, grabbed for my arm and forced it up behind my back. I kicked at him, but I couldn't twist out of his grip."

She looked up, tears streaming down her face. "I kept yelling for Finlay to stop hoping someone in the house would hear me. I begged and pleaded for them to let Andrew be, but I knew they wouldn't stop. I tried to lean over and grab the dagger hidden in my boot, but Torcall's hold was too tight. He kept me restrained and forced me to watch as Finlay smothered Andrew to death."

Freyja shook her head slightly then lowered her gaze to her hands, which lay lifelessly on her lap. "Once Andrew was dead, he tossed the pillow aside and came for me. I glared at him as I fought to get free so I could go to Andrew and maybe help him. I'm sure my expression held only a small amount of the contempt I felt for Finlay." Hugh's chest tightened, making it hard for him to breathe.

Freyja rubbed her hands over her face, as if trying to scrub the awful memories away. "I couldn't understand how a person could do such a thing to his brother." She clasped her hands into two fists. "I was so angry at him that when he stood in front of me, I kicked him as hard as I could between his legs."

Although Hugh's body jerked at the description of what she had done, his heart swelled with pride at her courage.

"Finlay doubled over in pain and swore. I fought against Torcall, but he twisted me aside to prevent me from kicking his master again. When Finlay finally stood, he was furious. He sneered at me and backhanded me across the face, promising that I had sealed my own fate.

She licked her dried lips then continued with her tale. "The sharp pain shot through my cheek and exploded in my head." She closed her eyes and rubbed the side of her face as if the strike had just occurred. "My sight blurred for a couple of seconds, and I tasted blood. Pain from the pressure on my arm and shoulder radiated down my back and spread throughout my limbs."

Hugh could not take any more. He shot to his feet and raked his fingernails through his hair as he paced the floor. "'Twas yer brother who beat ye then and abandoned ye in the woods to die?" He turned and saw the tortured sorrow displayed on her pretty face. The bruising on her face had faded but he would never forget how battered the poor lass had been.

"No." She shook her head, lifted her chin, and stared into the distance. "Finlay called his warriors in from the corridor and told them I had murdered *his* brother. Torcall and Dunn both attested to his lie. He instructed his men to take me to the great hall. He said, as acting laird, he would deliver my punishment immediately. I glanced over my shoulder at Andrew's lifeless body praying he would rise up and save me, but they dragged me out of his bedchamber and down to the great hall."

"Lass," Hugh whispered. He crossed to her chair and placed his hand on her shoulder. "If ye wish to stop and rest, ye can. I know this must be verra difficult to relive." His beautiful amber eyes revealed his deep compassion and concern, which encouraged Freyja to continue.

"I must go on. I want no lies between us either." She stood and wandered aimlessly around the room, all the while rubbing her hands up and down her arms. Hugh wanted to hold her, console her, reassure her that the men who did this to her would pay at the tip of his sword.

"Word of my arrest quickly spread throughout the castle and the hall filled with whispering clan members. Finlay sat in the Laird's chair at the high table on the dais as if he were king of Scotland. He wore my father's white fox robe draped over his shoulders." She scoffed with disgust and added, "To emphasize his power over the clan, he even wore his wig. Dunn and Torcall dragged me forward and forced me to stand before their master like a criminal.

"The room fell silent.

"Finlay stared at me, his beady little eyes full of contempt. His voice was loud and forceful when he spoke. 'Freyja,' he said, 'Ye hae been charged with murdering yer laird, our chieftain.' I heard a loud murmur fill the room. I struggled to get free. I yelled, this wasn't true and that he knew I didn't kill our brother. I told him that he couldn't accuse me or punish me for something he knew I did not do.

"Finlay raised his hands and solemnly said, 'These are sad circumstances, Freyja. You have suffered considerable losses in yer young life.' He scratched his chin as our father was known to do, then added, 'Which we all know can cause people to act out in ways we don't always understand. Everyone here knows how unpredictable and quick tempered you can be when you're angry.'"

Freyja crossed her arms and hugged herself, as if trying to gather up the strength to go on. Her heart pounded wildly in her chest. After a moment she whirled around to face Hugh, her hands fisted at her sides. "If I could have broken loose from those two smelly brutes, I would have shown Finlay how unpredictable I could be."

"I know ye would hae, lass."

"Then Finlay said, 'Since you are legally my sister, I feel I should be lenient toward you this day.'" Freyja strolled over to the window and glanced out. "Instead of hanging me or locking me in the dungeon, he said he would give me the appropriate funds to start my life over. Which of course were all lies to show his compassion to the clan. Then he banished me from the clan and from all Weir lands forever.

"When I declared that I hadn't killed Andrew, Torcall gagged me. He and Dunn dragged me from the great hall and bound me to the back of a saddled horse. Torcall felt under my skirts and found my hidden dagger and the knife from my boot." She paused before continuing. "He ran his hand higher up my leg in search of additional weapons. I would have spit on him if there hadn't been a filthy rag tied over my mouth." Her body trembled, but she forbade herself from crying.

Hugh slouched forward with his hand on the window casing; his head hung low as if he were deep in thought. Mayhap he couldn't stand to look upon her any longer.

"We rode from the castle at a gallop. I felt sick that I wasn't permitted to speak for myself, to explain what really happened. Though I know it would not have done me any good. I realize now that Finlay had planned to kill Andrew as soon as he found out Andrew was getting better. I believe my father and Andrew had the same illness, which no one had been able to name or cure."

She walked back to the chair and sat down. "It was well after the sun set when we finally stopped to let our horses rest. We had turned off the main road hours earlier, and I figured this must have been a shortcut to Edinburgh. Torcall pulled me from my horse and tossed me to the ground like a sack of grain as Dunn tended to the horses.

"Torcall removed his sword and several blades from his person and tossed them aside. He grinned at me and said he had been looking forward to this all day. I didn't know what he meant until he knelt down by my feet. When he grabbed for me I kicked him in the chest, but he quickly regained his stance. His large fist shot out and struck me in the side of my face, causing my head to snap back. I heard him yell for Dunn to come and help hold me down so he could lift my skirts."

She stood and flexed her arms and fingers, trying to relieve some of the unexpected tightness. "That was when I realized if I didn't fight back, I was never going to make it to Edinburgh alive. I kicked Torcall in the face and rolled across the ground. We were deep in the woods, and I couldn't see much past a few yards in front of me. I finally worked my hands free from the rope and pulled the gag from my mouth. I staggered to my feet and scanned the area. Years of fighting with my brothers and other lads had taught me where best to aim a punch and kick. I got several good hits in before they brought me down. I took more hits to my head, and my ribs and back, before I finally drifted off to a place, which promised everlasting peace."

Hugh crossed the room and wrapped his arms around her. When she leaned into him, he pulled her closer and stroked her back. He inhaled deeply and said, "Ye have occupied my mind every minute these past few days, wondering what was true and who ye really were. Noo I know what treatment ye hae had to withstand, it makes me furious. Believe me, I am going to keep ye at my side from this moment on." He kissed Freyja's brow, wrapped his strong arms around her and kissed her and kissed her soundly.

Freyja clung to him. Her feelings were growing ever stronger for Hugh. It was going to be more difficult to leave him than she had imagined.

Thirteen

When their long passionate kiss ended, Freyja was left struggling to catch her breath and unable to think clearly. She dropped her forehead onto Hugh's shoulder. She felt loved and protected when he held her in his strong arms. Could she turn her back on everything she knew to start a new life with him? Hugh's offer threatened Freyja's sense of duty, her obligation to avenge Andrew's death, and her responsibility to her clan to see Finlay and his goons punished.

Hugh kissed Freyja's forehead. "Ye think yer ready to face Laird Cameron and describe to him what happened, love?"

Freyja nodded slightly, as Hugh released her and crossed to the door. She shivered against the unexpected emptiness she felt at his parting. When the door opened, she heard muffled voices emanating from the corridor. She sat back down, her shoulders curl forward, and she clasped her hand together on her lap to keep them from trembling. Her body betrayed the warrior within, and she felt the frightened and wounded child in her emerge.

She'd thought by revealing what took place, she would feel unburdened and absolved of any wrongdoing. But what would happen to her if Laird Cameron didn't believe her innocent of doing her brother harm?

Everything is so confusing and unreal.

A moment later the laird entered the chambers. He appeared tight lipped and averted his gaze from her. Lady Adriana scurried along behind him as if trying to keep up with her husband's long stride. Hugh and Malcolm entered next, and Malcolm settled into the chair by the door. Laird Cameron's thick black brows were pulled together in a deep scowl. Lady Adriana reached for his hand, which vanished within his giant paw. She rubbed her other hand up and down his arm, eventually causing his expression to soften. He glanced down at his wife and smiled.

Once everyone was seated, Laird Cameron nodded his head toward Freyja and said, "Ye may commence." He glanced at his wife and paused. When he spoke again his voice was more tender. "Whenever yer ready, Miss Freyja ye may commence."

Freyja swallowed hard. She drew in a deep breath and began retelling her tale of the events from the day of Andrew's murder, up until she awoke in the hunting lodge next to Hugh. The three men sat devoid of emotions as she spoke. However, Lady Adriana's feelings were plain to see by her deep frown and the anguish in her eyes.

Freyja's hands shook, her throat felt dry. She glanced over at Hugh, and he nodded encouragingly. Laird Cameron listened intently, simply nodding as if unable to find the proper words to comment. By the time Freyja finished relaying the events of that horrible day for the second time, she was exhausted and unnerved.

Laird Cameron leaned forward and took Freyja's hands in his. When he spoke, his voice was slow and gentle. "I believe ye were in no way responsible for ye brother's death, lass. I shall take this information into serious consideration and devise a plan on how best to address Laird Weir. There is no need for ye to worry." He stood and offered his hand to his wife. "Come Love, I think ye best return to our chambers and rest."

Freyja watched the giant of a man she'd feared gently hug his weeping wife to his side and exit the chambers. When she glanced toward Malcolm at the door, the handsome soldier came to attention with his arms flat against his sides. He bowed respectfully, acknowledging her as a chieftain's daughter before turning on his heels and bolting from the room.

She relaxed back in her chair, and with great relief exhaled a long breath. She was proud of herself for not breaking down before the laird and her ladyship.

Hugh reached over and took her hand and looked deep into her eyes. "Ye astound me lass. I Cannae believe ye were able to tell the tale again without any trace of emotion."

"I just wanted to get it over with as soon as I could." She closed her eyes for a moment, then asked, "What do you think Laird Cameron will do?" She turned and looked at Hugh. "It was nice of him to offer to take care of the situation himself, but I'm worried in doing so, it might generate fighting between my old clan, people who I have known and loved all my life, with your clan, people I have grown to love and respect." Hugh stood, took her hand and helped her up from the chair. "You know," she added, "People on both sides will resent me for any deaths that might occur."

"Everything will be fine, love," he said, wrapping his arms around her. "My cousin will figure out what the best thing to do is. There is no need for ye to worry. Besides yer safe here with me."

True. Freyja knew if she stayed and married Hugh, she would have the protection of the MacCormac Clan. But what would happen to Sorcha who was still bound to marry Finlay? Sorcha would never be safe from Finlay and Freyja couldn't do that to Sorcha. However, when Finlay and his goons were punished for what they had done, she and Sorcha would be free to marry as they wished.

At the door, Hugh stood behind her and pulled her back against him and whispered, "We have a few hours afore dinner is served." His breath tickled her neck, sending shivers down her back. "I have an idea how we can pass the time."

Freyja leaned back against Hugh. "I would love to ride Saga before I wash and dress for dinner if you think there is time." She still hadn't found which field Saga was being kept in. Even though Laird Cameron believed her innocent of murder, there hadn't been enough time for him to decide what to do about Finlay. Something had to be done quickly. She couldn't put the lives of either clan in danger. She needed to venture to Dreki Craige Castle alone and deal with her brother and his men herself.

She glanced over her shoulder and noticed Hugh's frown. It was obvious he had something entirely different from riding horse on his mind.

~

Hugh and Freyja returned from their ride in time to ready themselves for dinner. Freyja offered only a quick thank you to Hugh before she raced up the steps and disappeared through the door into the castle. Puzzled, he watched her flee. She had been deep in thought during their ride, and when she had spoken, it had been to ask questions about their surroundings and how many kilometers it was to the MacCormac's northern border.

Later Hugh entered the great hall where several soldiers along with Cam and Malcolm where gathered near one of the long tables. Big Alec was in the middle of telling the story of Freyja's expert sword play in the training ring.

Why hadn't she told him about this when they were riding?

Then Alec said, "Robbie wanted to see the baby lambs, and so, Lady Adriana was taking him to the barns." Hugh noticed a couple of the younger soldiers were nodding in agreement as they listened. "As they strolled along," Alec continued, "Robbie ran ahead and disappeared behind the barn. No one realized the lad was in danger until Freyja ran after him. Her quick action saved him from a crazed wolf that threatened to attack the lad." Alec paused, then placed his hand on his sword and pulled it free. "The lass drew her sword and stood between the snarling wolf and little Robbie." He struck his sword out in front of himself, reenacting the attack. "Once Lady Adriana retrieved the lad Freyja backed up. As the lass turned to walk away, the wolf charged forward, knocking her off her feet. Quick thinking as she is, Freyja rolled onto her side and raised her sword, stabbing the wolf as it leaped toward her." The man pulled back his wide shoulders and proudly puffed out his chest. The great hall erupted in cheers.

Hugh wavered between being proud of Freyja and distraught after hearing her tale of what happened and how she ended up buried alive in the woods. And now this, he was sure she was the bravest woman he had ever met. He couldn't wait to be alone with her later. He had something very important to ask her.

Suddenly, the room grew silent. Hugh turned and followed the gaze of the crowd to four women who had just entered the hall. Hugh smiled at his Aunt Moira, fashioned in her finest gown, as if ready for an audience with the King. She could be an annoyance when meddling in his life, but she had been good to him and his cousins throughout the years. Lady Adriana and Miss Sorcha beautiful and demure, as always. They stood in the entry and waited as the crowd took them in. Hugh's breath caught in his throat at the sight of the fourth woman, the most beautiful woman he had ever seen. Freyja stood tall and exquisite in a mossy green dress with a scooped neckline, fitted tabbed bodice and bosque waistline. The quarter length over-sleeves and full skirt softened her muscular frame and accentuated her womanly curves. The green magnified the green in her eyes. Her long honey blonde hair had been pulled up and fashioned in large curls upon her head, and several strands curled along her slender neck. Two short strands of pearls hung around her neck, and she wore matching pearl earbobs. He had grown used to and quite enjoyed viewing her long muscular leg and firm bum in his trews. But her shapely body in a gown left a mystery as to what lie beneath the folds of all that material. Helping her with removing the gown would be like unwrapping a special gift—something he was looking forward to.

Several soldiers rushed to crowd around Freyja; they all seemed to be talking at once. Hugh slowly approached her, not quite knowing how to act around this new version of Freyja but he couldn't get close to her due to the other men demanding her attention.

With a wave of jealousy, Hugh shook off his hesitancy. He would take on all of the soldiers if that was what it would take to get her all to himself. Malcolm nudged Hugh's arm and handed him a bottle of brandy and said, "Yer gonna need several bottles to get through this night, cousin."

Hugh finally got close enough to overhear what was being said. He heard one of the young soldiers ask her about her training, and if she would practice with him sometime. She replied in a low, astonished voice, "Well, I have a couple of things I need to attend to, and I am not quite sure how much longer I will be here."

After a few moments, Cam stepped forward and broke up the crowd. He offered his wife his arm and escorted her to the high table. When the young soldiers hesitated, Malcolm, with a wide grin, stepped around the lads and offered Freyja his arm. Left holding the bottle of brandy, Hugh felt like a fool. Turning he noticed his aunt and cousin waiting to be escorted to their chairs. Hugh stepped to his aunt and offered her his arm. As he walked his aunt to her seat he heard a very unladylike snort behind him. Over his shoulder Hugh saw that after Malcolm had escorted Freyja to her chair, he had returned and offered his arm to Miss Sorcha. Tiny Sorcha came level with Malcolm's elbow. He held his head high and his elbow to match, which with Sorcha's straight black hair, made it look as if he held a large raven on his arm. Hugh glanced down the table to Freyja, hoping to get her attention, but she wouldn't acknowledge him. He set the bottle down on the table and sank into his chair. It was going to be a long night.

~

The sound of woman's laughter and vibrant voice drifted into the great hall seconds before a bonnie lass escorted by a very tall, thin young man with a thick head of wild red hair entered the great hall. The girl, about ten and six, floated into the hall as if the castle were her home. The girl waved to the high table, which was followed by Lady Adriana's squeals of delight.

Several of the young soldiers jumped up from their seats hoping to intercept the lass and battled to be the first to address her. Lady Adriana rose from her seat, clasped her hands together, and waited as the lass struggled to get through the throngs of young soldiers rapidly surrounding her.

Freyja watched in trepidation as Hugh, grinning ear to ear, slid his chair back and struggled to his feet. He cleared his throat and bellowed, "There's me beautiful lassie." He stumbled off the platform and lumbered to the girls' rescue. "Off with the lot of ye," he yelled, swinging his long arms threw the air shooing the other men away. It was obvious to Freyja that he'd had too much to drink.

He leaned down, wrapped his arms around the lass, and lifted the girl high into the air. Lady Adriana gasped and grabbed her husband's arm. The pretty little lass squealed with delight and laughed as Hugh swung her around in a circle. "Ah, love I hae missed ye." He stuffed his big face into the girl's neck and made a loud kissing sound. Freyja cringed; she'd had enough of Hugh's ridiculous behavior. She stood ready to leave or confront Hugh, but she hadn't decided which she would do when Lady Adriana reached over and placed a hand on hers and squeezed it gently.

Hugh set the lass back on her feet and released her to the scowling tall redheaded lad, who escorted the still laughing girl to the high table. The serious lad bowed before Laird and Lady MacCormac, then released the girl into Lady Adriana's arms. He turned and crossed to Big Alec, who stood behind the high table. Big Alec hugged the lad and thumped him loudly on the back. After a few words that Freyja couldn't hear, Alec left his station to the lad and joined his wife, Bethany at one of the lower tables.

After a lengthy hug, Lady Adriana turned to Freyja. "Lynette, may I introduce Freyja Weir of Clachan Craige. Freyja, this is my dear sister, Miss Lynette Boyd."

Freyja smiled as she spoke but wondered about the relationship between Hugh and this petite bonnie lass. "It is very nice to meet you, Miss Lynette. How wonderful that you could come for a visit, your sister was telling me earlier how much she missed you."

"It's my pleasure..." The lass replied then continued to speak but Freyja's gaze had locked with a set of smoldering amber eyes at the other end of the table. Hugh's intense stare sent shivers racing up her spine and she couldn't draw an intelligent thought. Nevertheless, she wasn't sure if his seductive stare was meant for her or the beautiful young lass seated beside her.

Lady Adriana ushered Freyja over one chair so she and her sister would be seated beside each other. Once everyone was seated, Lady Adriana motioned for the food to be served.

Miss Lynette rattled on excitedly and with great animation about a play she had seen in Edinburgh. Freyja feigned interest in what the girl was saying. Her thoughts wandered back to Hugh and what was possibly going through his mind. Then she heard Lady Adriana ask her sister about where their father was.

Miss Lynette sighed and replied, "Since I decided to stay

here with you for a week or two, Father went on home without me. You know how he likes the comfort of his own home."

Cam mumbled something under his breath which made Malcolm chuckle. Though Malcolm quickly added, "Not everyone enjoys staying within their own walls, Cam. I also enjoy going to Edinburgh and watching plays, amongst other entertainment."

Behind her, Freyja overheard Lady Moira reassuring Sorcha that Hugh would do his duty to the clan and marry who his laird instructed him to marry. Even though Sorcha appeared unconvinced, Lady Moira continued listing the many wedding preparations she felt still needed addressing.

She noticed that Hugh had settled back in his chair and refilled his glass. He paid no attention to the food nor his auntie or anyone else in the hall. Freyja thought she hoped Hugh would come to her chambers tonight, but now she wasn't sure it would be wise. She wondered if his persistent drinking meant he had resigned to the fact of marrying Sorcha. Besides, he had ignored her after she had donned the lovely dress Bethany had made especially for her.

Freyja thought there had been something special between Hugh and herself, but she must have been wrong. He had a duty to his clan and in doing so, must do as his laird commands.

She was so confused her head pounded. If Sorcha was still betrothed to Finlay, then why had she come there to marry Hugh? It was obvious Hugh had strong feelings for Lady Adriana's sister, Miss Lynette. The lass was beautiful, and it would be a good match.

Freyja told herself whomever Laird MacCormic deemed Hugh should marry, didn't affect her because she didn't care and wouldn't be here to witness either union.

Fourteen

Freyja merely picked at the food on her plate during the meal. Hugh admitted he hadn't eaten much either. Glancing at the empty bottle lying on the table before him, it appeared he'd drank more than enough brandy. A movement to his far right caused a mixture of panic and excitement as he watched Freyja excuse herself from the meal, and step down off the platform and head toward the corridor.

Hugh stumbled to his feet and heard Malcolm, next to him chuckle. With as much precision as possible, he stepped off the platform, collected himself and started to follow her. His quest was interrupted when he passed his auntie and cousin Sorcha, who were seated at the other end of the table.

"Hugh!" He heard his auntie's stern voice as she reached across the table as if to catch a hold of his tunic. "I wish to speak to ye."

Without turning his head to acknowledge her he said, "Not noo, Auntie," and continued walking.

"Ye cannot avoid me, lad. I'll seek ye out soon. Stubborn, brute."

He chuckled. Him a brute? His head felt as if a *brute* had sat on it. Once he reached the corridor, he headed for the stairs to the upper level. He hurried after Freyja hoping he wouldn't fall over and break his neck. He had to speak with her, ask her to marry him. Shaking his head he wondered why he had acted like such an eeejit when Miss Lynette arrived. He admitted he must have drank too much brandy, but only because of all the attention the young sods were paying Freyja when she'd entered the hall. She looked astounding, yet he hadn't been able to get close enough to tell her so. At last, he reached the upper floor. He sighed and exhaled a long breath before heading down the corridor toward her chambers.

~

Freyja kicked off her slippers. This miserable night had been a waste of time. Bethany had spent a considerable amount of time trying to transform her into an attractive woman in the new dress she'd made for her. Bethany even dressed her hair and added jewelry to help her look like a lady, and Hugh hadn't even approached her or spoken one word to her. Yet made a fool of himself fussing over the lovely lass, Miss Lynette with the big blue eyes.

Leaning down, Freyja took a chunk of wood out of the basket and tossed it into the hearth. Sparks danced up from the coals and the earthy smell of wood filled the air. She tossed two more chunks in the hearth, then lit the end of a long thin stick of wood and held the flame to a candle until it offered a measure of light.

She pulled the pins from her hair and tossed them on the dressing table; a soft knock sounded at her door. Freyja crossed to the door and pulled it open expecting to find Beathany there to help her undress. To her surprise, Hugh leaned against the doorframe and stared back at her through hooded eyes. The flames from the fire sparkled in his amber eyes. His hot gaze ignited tiny fires across her body as he inspected her from the top of her head to her bare toes poking out from under her gown.

"In that color of green with yer hair loose and hanging to yer hips, ye look like a goddess who materialized right from the sea, lass." He entered the room and closed the door, then pulled her into his arms and kissed her. "Yer lips taste of sweet berry wine," he whispered into her hair. "And ye smell of lavender soap."

She wanted to be angry with him, except his words and the depth of passion in his eyes were quickly melting the icy barrier between them. "I'd be thinken ye are a wee bit drunk, Laddy," she said in her best Scottish accent. He rubbed his hands slowly up and down her arms and chuckled at her teasing. A warm sensation engulfed her, sending shivers to the tips of her fingers.

"Aye, I hae drunk only enough to loosen thy tongue so I may say the things I wouldnae otherwise be able to express to a lovely woman such as yerself." His eyes twinkled with mischief and a wicked boyish grin slowly appeared on his tanned face. He kissed her again, and his hands made quick work of untying the laces on her gown. Soon the gown slipped off her shoulders and pooled around her ankles on the floor. He scooped her up into his arms as if she were no more than a sack of seed and carried her to the bed.

He laid her down and stretched out beside her and his lips were on hers again. Taking his time, he kissed a trail across her cheek and along her neck. Freyja reached up and slid her fingers through his beautiful, long, auburn hair. Without warning he pushed her on to her back and was straddling her, holding her arms out to her side. Freyja's heart raced and she started to panic. She didn't like being in such a vulnerable position and having her arms restricted. "There is no need for you to hold me down," she said.

"Ah lass, I admit I hae a burning desire to ravage ye, however, I'm afraid I'm in no condition to wrestle with ye tonight. I wish to take my time exploring yer glorious body and hear ye cry-out my name as I bring ye pleasure."

A wave of heat rushed up her chest to her face. "I... I wanted to please you," she said, embarrassed at her actions when they last made love. "I thought... I'm sorry if I did something wrong."

He smiled down at her. "Ye did nothing wrong, love. Ye surprised me that 'tis all." Freyja exhaled with relief.

"If ye can be still, I weel show ye a more enjoyable way of doing things." His lips brushed the corner of her mouth then ran his tongue over her lower lip. He continued until she opened her mouth and granted him access. He groaned and deepened the kiss.

Lying perfectly still, Freyja endured the wonderful torture his lips caused as they trailed down her arm. He licked and suckled the soft skin of the inner side of her elbow, then seized a pebble-hard nipple in his mouth. Freyja wanted to touch Hugh's head, shoulders, and back all at the same time. She was lost in the touch of his lips and hands as they roamed over her body. Right when she thought she was about to lose her mind, Hugh stood and removed his clothes.

His expression grew serious as he returned to the bed and snuggled up next to her. He gathered her into his arms, and he gazed down at her. "Stay here with me, lass—and marry me."

Stunned at his proposal, she blurted, "What about Sorcha and Lynette?"

Hugh pulled her closer and said, "What would I want with mere babes when I could hae ye, a woman." He moved above her and with his knee nudged her legs apart. Freyja's knees bent and he gently enter her. "Say that ye'll stay with me," he whispered in her ear. "Tell me ye *want* to stay and be my wife." He slowly pulled back and then pushed into her again.

Freyja was on the edge ready to fall. She slid her arms around his neck and fisted her hands into his hair. "I'll stay with you," she said, pulling him down until their lips touched again and his hard body covered hers.

Moments later, Hugh collapsed and rolled off to one side. Breathing heavy, he placed his forehead against hers, and whispered, "Ah, lass, ye've stolen my breath and my heart." He sighed and slipped off to sleep.

Freyja rolled onto her side. Yes, she had strong feelings for Hugh, but had she been wrong to agree to stay with him... Marry him? What about her family obligations? What would her late brother, Andrew, want her to do? Go after Finlay and avenge his murder, or would he want her to marry Hugh and have a real chance for happiness?

Worst of all, if she stayed and married Hugh and Finlay wasn't held responsible for his actions, Finlay would come for Sorcha, and the poor girl would be the next to suffer his cruelty.

There were more lives at stake here then just her own. Finlay truly needed to be delt with and the sooner the better.

The next morning Freyja's head ached from worrying all night if she had done the right thing by agreeing to stay with Hugh instead of focusing on her duty to avenge her brother's death. She'd slept late, so when she awoke Hugh had already left. Dressed in her familiar trews, boots, shirt, and leather jack, she entered the great hall. Lady Moira, Lady Adriana, Miss Sorcha, and Miss Lynette were gathered at one of the long tables, all speaking at once.

"We cannot go to the village without an escort," Lady Adriana said as Freyja approached the table. "Cam, Hugh, and Malcolm are gone out for a hunt. Big Alec is training men in the far east fields, and others are helping with hauling sacks of seeds to the fields to be planted."

"There are hundreds of men here," Miss Lynette said, confronting her sister.

"I have already told you, all of the men are out scouting, hunting, on guard duty or planting," Lady Adriana replied. "There really isn't any extra men available to escort us to the village."

"The village isn't far," Miss Lynette stated with frustration. "Besides, it's not as if we are planning on crossing any of MacCormac's borders. Obviously, we are safe on your own lands."

Freyja caught Sorcha staring at her. Sorcha grinned and said with a touch of sarcasm in her voice, "Freyja can escort us to the village. We certainly should be safe with her along to protect us. Especially after *killing...*" Sorcha paused and stared into Freyja's eyes as if challenging her. "That horrible wolf." Sorcha finished her sentence with the slightest smirk.

Anyone who *really* knows Freyja, would know they could easily be eliminated if they chose to challenge her." Sorcha kept eye contact with Freyja and raised her chin defiantly.

"That is a fantastic idea. Don't you all agree?" Miss Lynette said as she jumped up from the bench and clapped her hands together.

With a concerned expression, Lady Adriana approached Freyja. "What do you think, Freyja, the village isn't very far from the castle."

"You know better than I, milady. If you feel all is well with this arrangement, I will do as you ask." It would also provide the perfect opportunity for her to check out her surroundings.

Freyja saddled Saga. The stablemaster hitched a small cart to an old gelding, which Lady Adriana insisted on driving herself. Freyja trotted out ahead of the wagon and stopped at the gate to speak with the guard. The young soldier came to attention as she approached him.

"I am escorting Lady Adriana and these three women to the village. Inform Laird Cameron and Commander MacCormac to our whereabouts when they return."

"Aye, Miss Freyja," he responded respectfully with a slight nod.

At home at Dreki Craige Castle, the servants, soldiers, and even her brothers had referred to her only as Freyja. No one had ever addressed her as *Miss* Freyja or introduced her using her customary title, Freyja Weir of Clachan Craige. Whether dressed in trews or a gown, here Freyja had been shown the respect due a Laird's daughter and treated fairly instead of a nuisance. This acceptance made her sit taller in the saddle as they rode through the gates.

Every noise, every hare under a bush, bird in the sky didn't go undetected by Freyja. The tragedies in her life had forced her to become a fighter and later develop her skills suitable for a soldier.

They made their way to the village with no problems. Leaving the horses and the cart with the blacksmith at the end of town. As the women made their way along the narrow road to the first tiny shop, people stopped and stared. Freyja suspected most of the villagers knew who she was and that she had saved their next laird from a deadly wolf.

They stepped up onto the boardwalk and entered the first shop, which wasn't much larger than a hut. The shopkeeper appeared surprised and thrilled to see them. The older man's mousy-gray, shaggy hair and beard were dusted with sawdust and tiny wood shavings. Smiling broadly, he rounded a long table piled high with crates and baskets filled with chunks of wood. He bowed his head and said, "Milady, 'tis a pleasure to see ye again. I hope ye fair well." Although he smiled and spoke to Lady Adriana, his piercing gaze shot to Freyja. He reached into one of the many pockets on his leather apron and started to pull something out. Freyja stepped in front of the women and pulled out her knife. The man stepped back, a genuine smile appeared on his face, and he produced small carved, wooden wolf. "'Tis for ye, Freyja Weir of Clachan Craige." He stood tall and straight as he handed it to her. "A gift to show my appreciation."

Freyja stared at the wooden animal in her hand. The details and coloring were perfect; it looked as if it could be real. The man was an artist. She shivered recalling what happened and just how close the animal had been to her. She slid her knife back up her sleeve then turned to the man. She nodded. There hadn't been many opportunities in Freyja's life to thank someone, so it was difficult for her to say the words. He nodded back as if he understood her silence and all was well between them.

The women came forward. They marveled at the man's talent and made proper sounds of approval. They flocked to the shelves and baskets along the wall, which were filled with intricately carved animals, bowls and mugs, and other items. The women inspected each item closely and purchased several before they were ready to move on. Leaving the woodcarver's hut, they strolled on to the next shop.

As they walked Freyja observed the villagers with their baskets filled with freshly picked spring vegetables and bread. There were carts along the road that offered spinach, horseradish, broccoli, and mushrooms. Baskets were lined up and filled with squash, parsnips, leeks, and onions. A large man at the other end of town hocked both fresh and dried fish, razor clams, kale and chards.

The four women entered a shop, which seemed much too small for Freyja to wedge inside, so she chose to stand just outside the door. A mixture of odors filled the air causing her to think of her home. She longed to be back in the salty air on the northern coast. Yet, the merchants and villagers were friendly and had even offered Freyja samples of their wares. When the women came out of a shop, Freyja stuffed the last bite of a piece of bread and cheese into her mouth. Lady Adriana grinned and pointed to the other side of the road. Freyja nodded and escorted them through a maze of carts and chickens that filled the narrow road. A young boy of about six with a thick mop of auburn hair stopped and stared at Freyja. A look of wonderment and a touch of fear shown in his large round amber eyes. Freyja wondered if a son of Hugh would look similar. She smiled and winked at the lad. He appeared frozen where he stood, but then one side of his mouth hitched up in a crooked smile.

The women stepped off the walkway and strolled along the dirt trail toward the final shop. Broken furniture lined the front of the structure. The old building was the largest of all the shops. It was nestled underneath a grove of huge trees. Freyja was struck by an eerie feeling, and she gestured for the women to stop and let her enter first. Shafts of light showed through the dirt-streaked windows and open door, casting shadows across the piles of tables, trunks, and chairs. She surveyed the large room noticing a long worktable covered in tools, two other windows and a door along the back wall. A man in a long leather apron stood off to one side of the room. He nodded his approval as if her inspection of his dwelling had been a normal occurrence. Returning to the entrance, she ushered the four women into the interior.

Freyja was about to step out of the shop when she noticed a group of armed riders enter the village from the other end of the road. The villagers scrambled off the road in fear, disappearing quickly into the shops or between them. The men were close enough that Freyja recognized them as a group of her brother's best soldiers. They were most likely looking for either her or Sorcha.

Freyja claimed responsibly for these women. She would protect them to her death, which could easily happen if they were found. Several men dismounted and began searching each of the buildings on both sides of the road. Two men came out of the woodcarver's shop; their hands filled with hand carved items she was sure they hadn't paid for. Carts were flipped over, baskets kicked, the contents smashed. A chill went up Freyja's spine as she recognized the commander, Torcall's, voice as he yelled instructions, insisting the men hasten their search.

Freyja turned and beckoned the women to gather together. She searched their faces then ending on Sorcha's she broke the news, "Several armed riders have entered the village from the far end. They must not discover us. We need to find a place to hide until they have left."

Lady Adriana stepped forward and peered around Freyja.

"They wouldn't dare to harm any of us while in our own village." Lady Moira nodded her head in agreement.

"These are my brother's men," Freyja stated. "They would do a number of things others wouldn't. I assume they are searching for his betrothed, Sorcha, but they would not hesitate taking you *all* back to Dreki Craige Castle and hold you for ransom." She glanced again out the door. "I am sure; however, my fate would be much worse. If they find me, I will be killed instantly. None of us are safe." She was being blunt, but the women needed to understand the severity of what might happen.

The shopkeeper said, "Come." He gestured for them to follow him. Freyja peeked out the window to see how close the men were. They were exiting and entering the next few shops and making their way closer to them. The shopkeeper led the women to a corner where furniture had been piled high behind several crates.

Freyja eyed the pile warily. "There isn't time to move and restack everything. What is out behind this building?" she asked as she crossed to the back door, opened it and peered out.

"'Tis all woods," the shopkeeper replied.

"Good." Freyja ushered the women out. "Stay quiet and close together. Head into the woods and find places to hide." She turned back to the shopkeeper.

He nodded once. "Go. Be safe."

Freyja ran, following the other women. They ran quite a ways before stopping by a large pile of boulders and crouching down behind them.

Loud voices could be heard and what sounded like heavy items being thrown against the walls of the shop they had barely escaped. Freyja presumed one of the soldiers would open the back door to see if anyone was hiding behind the shop. She motioned for the women to stay where they were and peered around the boulders. She couldn't see any of the men in or around the old shop. Hopefully, no one had seen them exit out the back. She needed to get the women to one of the buildings the soldiers had already searched at the other end of the village. Behind each shop were piles of broken carts and crates, clumps of small trees and bushes, or barns that housed a variety of animals.

Freyja checked her surrounding again then waved for the women to run to her. They made their way back to the woodcarver's shop at the other end of the village. They should be safe there; her brother's men had already searched it. They entered the shop and found the woodcarver sitting on the floor against the wall. His carvings were scattered across the floor, and a chair and crate were broken. The man had a cut and bruised eye, nevertheless he smiled when he saw them. "As ye can see, the soldiers were already here," he said.

"How badly are you hurt?" Freyja asked as she turned and glanced out the window to check where the soldiers were. Lady Adriana knelt down beside the man. She ripped two long strips from her underskirt and started bandaging his wound. When she finished, he thanked her and let Lady Moira help him to his feet as Sorcha and Lynette stood back wide-eyed.

Freyja turned back and addressed the man. "We need somewhere to hide."

"Over here." He hobbled over to a corner of the room. "Ye can hide behind here." The women gathered together behind the crates, and he proceeded to stack more crates and baskets in front of them.

Freyja stayed back and watched through the window as the soldiers exit the last building, mount their horses, and rode out of the village. She finally released a long sigh. "It is all right; you can come out. It would seem they have left the village."

One by one the women appeared from behind the pile of boxes. Although the women were relieved and offered their appreciation to the old woodcarver, Freyja noticed a slight apprehension in their eyes. The women huddled together looking to her for further instructions.

"We will wait here," Freyja said, "Until they have put some distance between them and us." The women hugged and smiled reassuringly at one another.

Then suddenly, Freyja heard the sound of racing hoofbeats on this end of the road. "Hide," she whispered and waved the women back behind the boxes. "Be quiet and don't come out no matter what happens." The four women did as she commanded. Freyja glanced at the wounded woodcarver and ushered him toward the women. When he was huddled behind the crates, then packed baskets up around them until she could no longer see them.

The horses stopped outside of the shop. Time seemed to stand still as heavy footfalls on the walkway grew louder, until they stopped on the other side of the door.

Freyja drew in a deep breath and quietly slid her sword from the scabbard on her belt and drew her knife that was strapped to her arm under her sleeve. She stood ready to defend and protect the four women and the shop keeper.

Her heart slammed against her chest as the door handle rose, and the door inched open. She raised her sword and dirk, poised to attack.

When the door inched open, she advanced forcefully, utilizing surprise as a weapon.

"Easy noo, lass." Big Alec's voice, soft and slow, gradually penetrated the loud pounding in Freyja's ears.

Freyja blinked several times as she began to process what had happened. She glanced at the backsword still in her hand. There had been no impact. There was no blood. Big Alec stood to the side of the entry, unharmed. He must have let the door swing open; his large frame not crossing the threshold. His words were scrambled in her mind for a few moments before she could comprehend what he was saying.

"Breathe. Freyja, ye need to breathe, lass."

She drew in a breath, as instructed, and focused on the warrior's face. Little by little her mind cleared, and her arms lowered to her sides. "I could have killed you," she said, her voice not much more than a whisper sounded childlike in her ears.

A slow grin crossed the big man's face, and he said, "Nay, I donae think so. I saw ye through the window and knew better than to walk into yer clever trap."

She smiled in response to his false praise but was sure it resembled something closer to a sneer.

Big Alec ducked through the doorway and entered the shop, which forced Freyja to take a few steps back. His broad shoulders and considerable height filled the small interior. He took in his surrounding then leaned over and whispered by her ear, "Always watch your flank, soldier."

Fifteen

Freyja rode in silence alongside Alec back to Corell Castle. Of course, she felt relieved their adventure to the village had ended without incident, but she was also frustrated that Big Alec and his men had charged into the village to save them as if she lacked the skill to protect herself and four women. She had evaluated their situation and devised a plan to conceal the women. She had the problem under control.

By now the guards and everyone within the castle are probably aware we left the castle unescorted. Once Laird Cameron learns of our outing, there will surely be ramifications for putting his wife and the other women in danger.

Annoyed by the whole affair, Freyja squirmed in the saddle, dreading the forthcoming consequences.

"Yer quick-thinking led those women to safety, lass," Alec said, turning toward her. "Yer bravery and cleverness is to be commended." The big warrior nodded his head. "Ye possess qualities of a good soldier and leader."

Freyja nodded her thanks then glanced away, humbled by his praise. "I've never considered myself brave," she chuckled. "Honestly, I was too distracted to think about being brave."

Alec smiled at her. "Ye hae good instincts, soldier. With so many folks in the village today, there could hae easily been a blood bath. Yer clearheaded thinking certainly saved those lives this day."

"I did what I thought was best." Freyja felt heat rise up her neck to her face.

"Weel, ye were smart to tell the guards at the gate to inform the commanders of yer location as soon as they returned. Once we reach the castle I will leave and look for Laird Cameron, Commanders MacCormac and Hayword. They will dispatch more scouts and double the guards in case those men return."

If Finlay's soldiers return to Dreki Craige Castle without Sorcha, Finlay will come back here for her himself and he won't come alone; he will have his whole army with him.

As they approached the main gate to Corell Castle, Alec reined in his mount. He instructed his men to stay mounted and outside the gate. Freyja followed Alec into the outer bailey. He directed his attention on Freyja and said, "I am leaving the women in ye care. Make sure they get safely inside the castle and stress the importance that they stay within the keep." He nodded once and formally excused himself. "Freyja Weir of Clachan Craige."

Once again, she'd been addressed by her customary title. Freyja stared after the man as he rode back out the gate. Up until now she had considered herself only a guest here at Corell Castle. However, after being address with such respect by the man, she felt like she had been accepted as a soldier, an equal.

Freyja guided Saga over to where the women were being helped out of their wagon. She reined in her horse, dismounted, and handed her reins to the waiting stable boy. She crossed to Lady Adriana who spoke soothingly to the distressed women milling around her.

"How are you all fairing?" Freyja asked, joining them. They all nodded their reply though she could see they were flustered and still frightened.

"Oh, Freyja," Lady Adriana said as she reached out and

wrapped her arms around Freyja engulfing her in a tight hug. "I am so happy you were there to protect us. I do not know what would have happened if those soldiers had found us."

Admiration and thankfulness shown in her ladyship's eyes, made Freyja feel like she'd been kicked in the gut. She had put the Laird's wife, his auntie, his distant cousin, Sorcha and sister-in-law in danger. Freyja realized if she had taken a moment to think of the consequences of escorting the women to the village alone, as a true soldier would have, they would have never found themselves in such a life-threatening situation. She may have acted bravely when danger first arose, but a good soldier would have anticipated the possibility of trouble before setting out on such a journey. With a pounding in her head and her stomach twisted in knots, Freyja tried to shake off the self-loathing that washed over her. She was still responsible for seeing the women safely into the keep.

She forced a smile and said, "Let me help you get everyone into the castle and settled." The woman's smile was slight, but she agreed and let Freyja usher her and the others toward the keep. Before reaching the steps, Lady Adriana glanced up at Freyja. Her eyes were large and round, she whispered, "A cup of tea with a drop or two of whisky will set everything right again."

Freyja patted the woman's shoulder. "All will be well, milady. You need to promise me that you will make sure you all stay inside until we know those soldiers have gone."

"Yes. Yes of course." She drew in a ragged breath. "Thank you for keeping us safe. And I speak for all of us when I say we are grateful to you for your quick actions today."

"Certainly, now off with you." Freyja gave her a nudge then watched the four women shuffle off in the direction of the keep. She was relieved everyone was safe but doubted Laird Cameron was going to feel grateful for her behavior.

Loud voices of men yelling caught Freyja's attention. Turning in the direction of the noise she saw men hurrying toward the gate, some climbed the stone steps to the battlement, while others disappeared into the barracks to collect their weapons. Through the gates she could see Laird Cameron, Hugh, Malcolm along with several other men mounted and facing the road. Scurrying to the wall she leaned against it hoping to keep out of sight as she inched closer to the gate. She squeezed in between the men and watched the riders approaching. They were the same men who were in the village earlier. Her brother's soldiers. She stepped back not wanting to be seen.

They rode close enough to the castle entrance so their voices could be heard. The commander of the troop of soldiers yelled, "Good day, Larid Cameron MacCormac." Freyja shivered at the sound of Torcall's voice. "We hae been informed Lady Sinclair and Miss Sorcha Sinclair are within yer walls," he stated. "Laird Finlay Weir has instructed us to retrieve his betrothed, Miss Sorcha and her aunt, and deliver her to Dreki Craige Castle."

Laird Cameron's horse pawed the ground, ready to charge forward if given the command. The MacCormac chief never looked more like a black giant than he did right that moment as he sat upon the back of a huge black stallion.

"The Sinclair women and their escorts will stay here until their visit is complete. If Miss Sorcha wishes to send a dispatch to Weir, I will hae a messenger ride north and deliver it to him," he replied, in his deep menacing voice. A couple of the men around her chuckled at his response. More clansmen gathered in around Freyja.

"Laird MacCormac," Torcall yelled. "Ye donae understand milord." He glanced around and Freyja ducked her head down, hoping he didn't see her. Returning his gaze to Laird Cameron, he yelled, "We donae intend on leaving without the lass."

Freyja heard the sound of horses approaching. Glancing around the soldiers and workers in front of her, she saw Big Alec and his men appeared off to the side of the gate. Looking up, she could see the men on the wall raising their weapons. Without warning, the Black Giant's voice boomed like a cannon, causing Freyja to jump. "While the Sinclair's and their escorts are behind my walls they shall be protected by the MacCormac Clan. Ye may deliver that wee bit of information to Weir yerself, *laddie.*" The last part was said with malice.

A deafening roar of laughter erupted and a young soldier standing next to Freyja clapped her on the shoulder and grinned. Over the lad's shoulder no fewer than fifty, heavily armed, mounted soldiers, waiting for the command to ride out. Torcall was outnumbered and most likely disturbed by those odds.

Her gaze shot back to Torcall. He seemed to realize he wasn't being taken seriously and was being dismissed, because he yelled, "We will return, MacCormac." Then he jerked on the reins making his horse rear. He spun the animal around and they raced off.

Freyja sighed with relief while everyone else laughed and glad-smacked each other on the back. The riders who had been waiting in the outer bailey were called out. Freyja watched the proud soldiers ride out through the gate. She knew Finlay wouldn't be happy when Torcall returned without Sorcha. Was Finlay foolish enough to return with the rest of his army and attempt to fight The MacCormacs? If that were to happen, many soldiers on either side would be killed. She had to do something to stop this disaster from happening.

Freyja made her way along the side of the wall and peered out the gate. She spotted Laird Cameron, Hugh and Big Alec still mounted. The scowls on their faces suggested Alec had told them about what happened in the village. Whirling around she disappeared into the large crowd gathered in the bailey and raced off in the direction of the keep. It was time for her to collect her thoughts and prepare for the unavoidable confrontation with Hugh and Laird Cameron.

Or better yet, with the bailey filled with clansmen and villagers mingling and celebrating the minor victory, now would be the perfect time for her to slip away unnoticed.

~

Covered in dirt and sweat and spattered with blood from the deer he'd shot while hunting, Hugh headed for the keep. His stomach growled like an angry dog as he crossed the outer bailey. Although Alec had reassured him Freyja was fine after the events of the morning, he needed to see the lass for himself. According to Alec, the near meeting with Weir's soldiers could've easily become disastrous.

Why would she put herself and the women of his family in danger by taking them into the village unescorted by guards. Wasn't getting beat and left for dead enough proof to her that she wasn't safe alone? What had she been thinking?

Hugh weaved in between and around numerous soldiers, castle workers, and villager celebrating. Women handed out mugs of ale to the men while stable boys hastily unsaddled the horses and put them away. The outer bailey was in the throes of joyful chaos. A soldier raised his mug and cried out, "Praise to our laird and chieftain, *The Mighty MacCormac!*" Another soldier yelled, "And to *Freyja The Warrior.*"

The bailey soon filled clan members raising their mugs of ale and chanting their praises.

As if his cousin could sense his thoughts, Cam appeared at his side. "When ye go to seek her out," he said in a formidable voice. "Bring her to my office."

Cam appeared disgusted by the celebration taking place in the yard behind him. They both knew it was a temporary victory and wouldn't be the last time they would hear from Laird Weir. Before Hugh could discuss the incident, his cousin had trudged away.

~

Even though it's the laird's duty to punish Freyja for her recklessness and poor judgement, Hugh expected Cam wasn't looking forward to it. He wished Cam would discuss what type of punishment he planned to administer with him first. Freyja would not have taken the woman into the village if she hadn't thought she was strong enough to protect them. Yet he knew her wounds weren't healed enough to withstand the lash or to spend several nights in the damp, musty dungeon.

Sorcha! He'd spotted her too late. Holding her skirts up and looking distraught, Sorcha-the-small-one, scurried toward him. Once she reached him, she flung her arms around his middle. "It was horrible," her voice trembled as she spoke. "I was so scared we were all going to die." Sorcha laid her cheek against his chest. "We should have never gone to the village on our own." Surprised by the girl's reaction, Hugh patted her awkwardly on the back. "Yer all right noo, lass. Yer weel protected within these walls."

"Oh, I am so happy you have returned to protect us." She glazed up at him and blinked several times.

"Aye," his voice sounded flat. Over the top of her head, Hugh scanned the area and spotted a group of men watching them with questionable expressions. Grabbing Sorcha by the arms, he gently set her back. "As I said, yer safe, noo. And ye should be inside the keep. Come, I will take ye in." She grinned up at him with what he considered to be misplaced admiration. Cupping her elbow, he steered her toward the keep. Another group of soldiers ambled in their direction, their brows raised as if questioning his intentions. Hugh prompted Sorcha to walk faster. Glancing back over his shoulder he noticed the first group of young soldiers had joined the other group. Not wanting to be confronted by them with Sorcha by his side, Hugh urged her forward, up the steps, and into the keep. Once inside he stopped and listened. Hearing Adriana's and his aunt's voices wafting down the corridor from the ladies parlor, Hugh guided Sorcha in that direction.

"Hugh. Please," Sorcha panted. "I cannae walk as quickly as yerself." She jerked her arm free of his grip.

Hugh came to a halt and peered over his shoulder. She smiled sweetly up at him then skimmed her hands down the front of her skirt. He released a long audible sigh. He didn't have the time to deal with Sorcha's childish games while he worried about Freyja and the punishment Cam was about to deliver to her. "Sorcha," he said, abruptly. "There is important business that needs my attention, so I would appreciate it if ye'd make an effort to walk faster." He offered her his arm, and when she slipped her hand around his elbow, Hugh started down the corridor.

Hugh stopped at the threshold of the ladies parlor. He searched the room and spotted the of women gathered together by the large window. Avoiding their curious stares, he trekked across the carpeted chambers and stopped. "Here 'tis one more for tea." Without waiting for a response, he nodded respectfully, turned on his heels, and quickly exited the room. A sick sensation twisted in his gut as he hurried in the direction of Freyja's chambers.

What if something had happened to her this morning? He should have been there to protect her.

Sixteen

Freyja paced back and forth in front of the hearth in her chambers replaying the events of the day once again in her mind. How could she have been so irresponsible as to put those women in such danger? She rubbed her at the pounding behind her temples. The appreciation in Lady Adriana's eyes haunted her, making her feel ill. If she had simply considered the consequences if something were to happen, she wouldn't be in this fix now. A good soldier would have anticipated the possibility of trouble before setting out on any journey alone.

She stopped at the window and gazed out. The sun had made its way across the sky and would soon descend and vanish into the sea. Mayhap she should have left when the commotion started in the bailey, but she wouldn't run from her responsibilities. She would accept what was due her.

Spinning away from the magnificent view she lumbered across the room with her hands swinging at her sides. She'd gone over every detail again, trying to discover a more skillful way to have protected the women. Gripping her the front of her waistcoat with both hands, Freyja gave it a quick jerk, then tugged on her open collar. She had decided to stay dressed as a soldier for when Laird MacCormac summoned her. She would not present herself before the laird wearing a gown covered with ribbons and bows as if she were a powerless woman. She had acted as a soldier, and she'd be damned if she wouldn't take her punishment as one. Damn Finlay and his men for destroying her life yet again. The mere thought of her brother made her blood boil. She glanced around, her chambers suddenly felt confining. Her hand went to the hilt of her sword.

What I need is an hour in the training ring to release some of this frustration.

A knock sounded at her door. Freyja stood frozen in place. This would be her summons to his lordship, who was waiting to hand down her well-deserved punishment. She drew in a deep breath and slowly exhaled. Chin held high, Freyja crossed to the door and pulled it open.

Hugh stood before her, his eyes inspecting every inch of her body, from the top of her head to the tip of her scuffed up boots. He stepped into the room and kicked the door closed. The tenseness in his shoulders seemed to ease. With a slight smile he said, "Lass, I worried so." He approached her, his arms reaching out as if to embrace her.

Freyja stepped away to avoid his touch. "Do you expect me to welcome your affections while I'm waiting to find out if your Laird intends to throw me in the dungeon?" Freyja stared back at Hugh, then brushed her long braid over her shoulder.

His brows dipped together, he exhaled loudly and stepped forward. "From what Big Alec reported happened in the village, ye acted swiftly and were able to keep yerself and the women hidden from the soldiers. He said ye had pulled yer knife and sword and were even ready to fight him."

"I didn't know who was on the other side of the door," she replied and turned away from him. Was he able to understand her embarrassment at finding Big Alec standing there, aware of her intentions?

She heard his boots scrape across the stone floor as he closed the distance between them. "'Twould hae been grand to witness the man's expression when he saw ye prepared to defend yerself. 'Tis happy I am, that none of ye were hurt today." He paused as if he expected her to turn and face him, but then he added, "I know ye thought ye could protect four women and yerself, lass." He reached out and took her hand in his. "Except next time I would hae ye wait for me so I might ride with ye."

Freyja spun around and faced him. Jerking her hand back from his, she spat, "I need no nursemaid to tend me." She was ready to continue but he stood so close. She noticed the dried blood speckled across his face and clothes, the scent of blood, sweat, and horse on his body. He truly was a warrior. She saw no malice in his amber eyes, only concern and affection for her, and empathy for her lack of wisdom and skill to protect herself. The last thing she needed or wanted was to be pitied by anyone.

"Laird Cameron wishes to see ye in his office." He spoke in low gentle tones. From his expression, Freyja knew he had come to collect her, and, in a few moments, she would learn what Laird Camerson thought her punishment should be for putting his wife and family members in danger. She held her head high, and exited her chamber, passing silently by Hugh.

As she approached the Laird's office, she saw Malcolm had once again been positioned outside the door. He jumped to his feet, knocked once, then opened the door for her to enter. Hugh had entered the office right behind her. Freyja stopped and stood at attention in front of the laird's desk. Striving to hold on to an amount of control, she stared at the large map hanging on the wall behind the desk. The laird glanced up from his papers and studied her.

"Before I hand down any punishment, I require yer perception of what took place before ye left the keep, up to the point when ye returned," Laird Cameron said. He leaned back in his chair and crossed his thick arms over his chest.

"Milord," she said, hoping her voice didn't reveal her

nervousness. "I felt confident protecting the women and myself while we traveled to the village. I was unaware Laird Weir had soldiers searching for his betrothed, Miss Sorcha. He must have sent soldiers to Sinclair Castle only to learn that she and Lady Moira had traveled to Corell Castle. If I had any idea that any form of danger could get by your border-guards and enter your land or the village, I assure you, I would have never permitted the women to leave the safety of the keep."

I did not get a count of how many riders entered the village, although I recognized many soldiers from the Weir Clan. As they searched every building on the south end of the village, we slipped out the back door of the old shop on the north end of the village. I instructed them to run into the woods and hid amongst the trees or anything they could find. We then made our way south to the shops the soldiers had already searched. When the soldiers were unable to find us, they left the village on the road heading east." Freyja swallowed and took another breath and continued. "But then I heard horses approaching again and presumed they were returning. By then we were in the woodcarver's shop. I instructed the women and the woodcarver to hid behind a pile of crates in the far corner of the shop. And when I heard footsteps on the walkway on the other side of the door and prepared myself."

Without uncrossing his arms, Laird Cameron raised two fingers signaling he had a question for her. "Alec tells me ye drew yer sword and knife and were about to fight him when he appeared before ye."

"If the soldiers from..." She paused and swallowed hard. "From the Clan Weir had found us, they would have killed me and taken the others back to Dreki Craige Castle to be held for ransom."

The Laird seemed lost in thought as he scratched his jaw. Anxious to have this over with, Freyja wished he would be quick with revealing her punishment. Her muscles tensed and it felt as if they were going to rip through her skin. She tried to stand still, to stay silent in hopes of not making her circumstances worse.

"Milord." She stood ridged, chin held high and said, "I acted as a soldier; therefore, I insist you present me with a punishment you would bestow on any other soldier."

Laird Cameron eyed her closely, as if assessing her merits. From behind her, she heard Hugh take a step forward. Laird Cameron raised a single thick black brow and shot Hugh a look, cautioning him to be still.

"Ye arrived at Corell Castle as a guest, Miss Freyja. Yet, ye have chosen to act and dress as a soldier. Therefore, I acknowledge ye as a soldier and will consider an appropriate punishment." He paused for a moment, then asked, "Do ye feel yer brother will return with his army, or do ye feel his commander was merely bluffing?"

Freyja sighed. She thought she knew Finlay; however, she would have never guessed him capable of killing Andrew or of throwing her out to those pigs and letting them do what they will to her. Freyja's eyes welled up with tears and her jaws ached from clenching them tightly. "I think Finlay has proven he is capable of doing anything to get what he desires. He has a strong army of about three hundred men. Once he learns Sorcha is here, he will come for her."

Laird Cameron's face held no expression. Leaning forward, he placed his scarred hands on the desk. When he stood, he towered over her. "After what happened to Laird Andrew, I expected what ye might say. Ye are excused for today. Report back to me in the morning. And Freyja, stay within the keep."

Freyja bowed her head, turned and exited his office, relieved to be leaving, but annoyed about having to wait until the morning to learn her fate. As she walked out, she heard the laird tell Hugh to stay.

~

Hugh watched his cousin as Cam paced around the office. "What do ye think about what she said happened in the village?" Hugh asked, sinking down onto a chair by Cam's desk.

Cam stopped and glanced over at Hugh. "'Tis the same story that Adriana told me. Except for the part where Weir's men apparently crossed our borders without being seen. Best post more patrols and tell them to expect more riders."

"Aye, I sent more patrols out after Weir's men left." Hugh wondered how they got past the guards that were already posted.

His cousin returned to his desk and sat down. "Good. Send Malcolm into me when ye leave." Hugh nodded. He understood Cam had a lot to think about, and he longed to spend more time in Freyja's company, so he left without question.

~

Freyja sat by the hearth gazing into the glowing flames. What was her punishment to be? The sun had sunk into the sea some time ago, and the supper Bethany had brought up to her earlier sat untouched on the table. She pulled her robe tighter, retying the cloth belt, and wondered how her life had become such a tangled mess in a short period of time. She stood and rubbed her temples as she wandered around her room. So much had happened in the span of a few days that she was now confused as to where her loyalties should lie. One moment she wanted to avenge Andrew's murder and what was done to her; the next, she wanted to forget all the pain and suffering and start a new life here with Hugh. Deep down in her soul she knew she couldn't let Finlay go unpunished for his deeds. If for no other reason than the safety of her clan, Finlay needed to be imprisoned for the murder of their laird. However, now, she was less enthusiastic about facing and fighting her brother. It seemed that her bloodlust had lessened, and she only wanted peace. This turn of perspective left her feeling guilty, as if she were abandoning Andrew and her clan.

She scrubbed her hands over her face. She needed a sign to point her in the proper direction and help her do the honorable thing.

Her thoughts were interrupted by gently knocking. Freyja crossed the room and opened the door. Hugh stood on the other side. He'd washed up and changed his clothes and probably had eaten his dinner.

"Good evening, lass. May I enter?" he asked with a somber expression.

Maybe he could help her decide what was best to do. She stepped back. "Aye, of course you may."

He entered her bedchamber and reached for her hand. "Do you know what my punishment will be?" She searched his worried expression for any clues of what to expect.

Hugh raised her hand to his lips and brushed a light kiss over her knuckles. "Nay. Though I expect he shall make an example of ye to the younger, inexperienced soldiers." He pulled her into his arm and nuzzled her neck, as he threaded his fingers through her loose hair. "If ye were to have come to Cameron dressed as ye are noo with yer hair down, he may have lost his mind as I do when I see ye so and let ye go unpunished." He kissed her neck and then stepped back. He stared into her eyes and said, "But nay. Yer a stubborn lass who showed up dressed as a man, demanding to be treated as one. So, noo yer forced to wait."

She pushed away from Hugh. "Would you have me stand before your laird as a simpering woman with bows and flowers in my hair?" She turned away from him. She couldn't tolerate the pity she saw in his eyes. "I trained to be a warrior." She spun back around and faced him. She could feel her face flush with anger. "I may be a woman, but I will not use that as a shield to hide behind. My honor demands if I chose to be a warrior, I be accepted and treated as a warrior."

"Aye, lass... Freyja. 'Tis that I am sorry for not being here so I could hae gone with ye to the village," he said.

"So, you think I am unable to protect four women and

myself? That I had need of your assistance and constant protection?"

"Nay. 'Tis not like that. I'm saying had I not gone hunting this morning, I could hae gone with ye and protected all of ye, then ye wouldnae be in a fix noo."

Freyja glared at him. She knew what he was saying, yet it still sounded like an insult to her.

"Lass, I dinnae come here tonight to do combat with ye." He wrapped his arms around her and slowly stroked her back. "I hae come to make love to my beautiful woman who has been many things. A Fallen Angel, the Greek Goddess, Athena, the Fearless Warrior Freyja, and the lass who sets my loins a blaze."

Freyja's anger melted from the fire in his eyes. She wrapped her arms around his neck and leaned forward and kissed him. With his arms wrapped tightly around her, she felt loved. The passion in his kiss promised a long night of love making. Was this the sign she waited for? Would a lifetime in his arms be her reward for letting everything else go? Maybe she could leave her old life and start fresh here with Hugh.

"Oh, lass, yer kisses set my blood to boil. 'Tis glad I am that I returned to see ye had a proper burial."

Stunned at his statement, her body stiffened. "What do you mean returned?"

He nuzzled her neck then kissed the tender skin above her breast. "Weel, when I first found ye I knew ye wouldnae hae made it to the castle alive." He opened her robe, slid her gown off her shoulder, and kissed her exposed flesh.

Freyja leaned back making him stop and glared at him.

His brows rose and he looked confused. "You said that you returned to bury me." She heard the devastation in her own voice.

"Aye," he nodded his head. "When I first came across ye in the woods, I decided 'twould be best to let ye rest in peace, instead of causing ye more pain by trying to move ye."

"How long was it before you returned for me?"

She couldn't believe what he was telling her. "Oh. I donae know," he sighed, kissing his way up to her ear. "Couldnae hae been more than four hours."

Freyja's hands slid from his shoulders and dropped to her sides. She couldn't imagine that he had been so heartless to have left her alone in the woods to die instead of taking the chance that she would survive the journey to Corell Castle. Yes, he'd come back, but to see her properly buried. He hadn't raced back distraught about not taking her with him earlier and praying she still lived.

The man she thought she knew would never have left her to die alone in the woods. Yet, he had. Did she really know Hugh? Did any person ever truly know another? Her father an Andrew were gone, Finlay was capable of murder and Duncan was a mere lad, and now Hugh. Oh, Hugh. How could you have betrayed me like that? She bit the inside of her cheek holding in her emotions. Was she to live her life without being able to trust or count on any man she allowed to get close to her? If he hadn't come back to bury her, he would have never known she hadn't died yet. Would she have frozen to death before the animals in the woods found her? Hugh, more so than Finlay, or Torcall would have been responsible for her slow and torturous death.

She tried to turn away from Hugh, so he wouldn't see the tears forming in the corner of her eyes, but he slid his arm around her middle and said, "Ah, Freyja, ye know how I feel about ye." He glanced down at her breasts, grinned and added, "And how much I want ye."

"I need to retrieve another blanket from the trunk." She said more to herself than him.

He pulled her close and whispered, "Let me warm ye, lass."

Freyja's head spun. Earlier she'd been convinced she should stay and start a new life, but now, guilt for not avenging Andrew's murder and leaving her clan under Finlay's rule, gnawed at her integrity. The revelation of Hugh's betrayal was the push she needed; the sign to return to Dreki Craige Castle.

Yet, she knew what she would be giving up when she left here, left Hugh. She loved him, but her obligation to her clan ran strong and deep. She let Hugh lead her to the bed and strip off her robe and night gown. She would let herself enjoy being in his arms one last time before she return home to make things right. Or die trying.

Seventeen

He released a satisfied groan as he awoke. The late morning sun streamed through the windows, indicating he'd slept soundly. Their love making had lasted deep into the night. Smiling, he rolled onto his side expecting to find Freyja beside him just as content, but she wasn't there. He sat up and glanced around the empty chamber.

He inhaled deeply then exhaled. *Poor lass must be famished after last night,* he thought to himself. His stomach rumbled. "Aye. All right." He laughed, then stood up and scratched his chest. The sun was high in the sky, telling Hugh he was about to miss another meal if he didn't get dressed and hurry below.

Hugh entered the Great Hall and searched for Freyja as he strolled toward the high table where Cam and Lady Adriana were seated. He continued his search as he settled onto the chair at Cam's right. "Hae ye lost something?" Cam asked, one thick brow raised as he studied Hugh.

"'Twould seem I hae missed sharing this meal with Freyja. How long ago did she leave the hall?"

Cam frowned. "I hae no seen her this morning." He turned to his wife and asked, "Love, Hae ye seen Freyja today?"

"No. I don't think she's come down yet. I have been here for quite some time, entertaining your son, and haven't seen her."

Hugh's gaze floated over the people gathered for their midday meal. At the far end of the hall, he noticed Maddy and a young serving girl having a serious conversation about something. Maddy's hands were fisted on her hips as she appeared to be scolding the lass.

The girl held a trencher piled with food and followed Maddy across the room. They paused to speak with another lass before approaching the dais and placing the large wooden tray on the table.

"Maddy," Hugh said, leaning forward on his elbows. "'Tis something amiss?"

"'Tis nothing ye need be worrying aboot, lad," she answered with less cheerfulness than usual.

"Is there something wrong, Maddy," Lady Adriana asked the cook.

"Nay, Milady," Maddy said, turning her head. "Nothing really." Maddy gripped her apron in her hands.

"Maddy," Cam's voice rumbled when he spoke, and the little cook jumped. "Tell me. What has yer feathers all ruffled up?"

"'Tis a matter of some missing food from the kitchen." She glanced from Cameron to Adriana. "I wonder if either of ye gave someone leave to take food earlier this morning?"

Hugh listened as he picked a piece of smoked fish and a hunk of cheese from the tray.

Cam leaned forward in his chair. "What time do ye think the food went missing?"

She wrung her hands together as she appeared to figure the time in her head. "'Twould hae been around three O'clock I think, cause I brought the bread in from the back kitchen around half past two and wrapped the loaves in cloths to stay fresh. I returned at five to prepare the meat to be roasted today and found a loaf of bread and four strips of dried meat missing.

Oh! And there was an empty biscuit tin left on the shelf in the pantry."

Hugh continued to eat, but Cam turned to Kinny standing guard behind them. "Kinny." The tall lanky lad stepped forward. "Check with the guards on duty last night. Find out if anyone noticed anyone sneaking around or if there is anything to report."

"Aye, Milord." Kinny nodded, turned and headed across the hall to do his Laird's bidding.

Hugh turned his gaze to his cousin, and asked, "What are ye thinking might hae happened during the night?"

Cam shook his head. "I cannae say, but I hae my suspicions." He turned his attention back to Maddy. "Maddy, check with the maids to see if they have found anything else seems amiss this morning. And thank ye for informing me if this. Times are hard and we need to keep an eye out for any vagabonds or beggars lurking aboot."

"Oh. Aye, Milord." The cook turned and scurried away.

Cam leaned back in his chair. He paused for a moment and regarded Hugh, then asked, "So, when did ye last see Freyja?"

Hugh's chest tightened. He contemplated punching his cousin in the nose but thought now was not the best time. It would be safer to share his thoughts instead. "So, noo yer thinking the lass has turned to steeling from ye after ye fed and clothed her." How could Cam accuse Freyja of such a thing?

Besides, she wouldn't leave him after the night they shared.

"I asked ye *when* mon," Cam demanded.

"'Twas maybe two," he replied offended by Cam's insinuations. Hugh pushed his chair back, causing it to tip over and crash to the floor. Hands clinched, he jumped off the platform. The first place he'd look would be the stables to see if Saga was gone. He'd prove his cousin wrong soon enough.

As Hugh headed out of the keep and down the stone steps, he replayed their conversations from the night before. She'd asked if he knew what her punishment might be. Cam's threat of punishment could have driven her away. There was no other reason for her to leave.

Hugh marched across the bailey toward the stables. He eyed the empty paddock where Saga had been placed yesterday as he passed by. Entering the stables he grabbed the first stable boy he saw by the back of the neck. "Where is the dapple-gray palfrey mare, Saga?"

The boy stared up at Hugh, his toes barely touching the dirt floor, his eyes bulging from their sockets. The lads voice shook when he replied, "I donae know. The mare was nay in the paddock when I went to bring her inside to feed her." Hugh set the lad back down and he dashed off.

He ambled out into the sunlight. His gaze swept over the outer bailey then paused when they came to the Barracks. Trotting across the yard, he prayed he was wrong as he entered the weapons room. The newest guard, Angus stood off to one side of the room scratching his head. He turned and stared at Hugh for a moment, looking to see if he held anything in his hands. "I donae understand it," he said, shaking his head. "There's a targe and a bedroll missing."

"What time did ye come on duty this morning?" Hugh asked the lad.

The young soldier scratched the back of his neck. "'Twas two o'clock. I counted everything when I came on, and I was noo counting afore I seek my bed." He shook his head again and added, "I swear on my sweet, sainted mum, I never heard nor saw anyone come in or ride out during the night."

Hugh's stomach dropped. He swallowed hard as the truth sunk in. Freyja was gone. Somehow, she'd snuck into the weapons room and grabbed a targe and a bedroll, then rode Saga right out the front gate without anyone noticing. Where would she have gone? She'd agreed to stay and marry him. Why would she have left him without a word?

He turned and stormed out of the building and almost ran into Cam. "What did ye learn?"

"Her horse is gone." He replied, moving away from Cam. He wanted to be alone to try and sort this out, not be asked questions he couldn't answer.

Cam reached for Hugh's arm. "Do ye hae any idea where she might be headed?"

Hugh stopped and faced his laird. "I believe she is headed to Dreki Craige Castle."

Cam jammed his fists on his hips. "Why would she go there? Why jump straight back into the fire after only recently healing from their last encounter?"

Looking Cam in the eye, Hugh said, "I dearly hope I am mistaken but, I think her plan is to confront her brother aboot murdering Laird Andrew, and for what his men had done to her."

Cam rubbed his forehead. "What could she possibly be thinking would come of that?"

"I fear she hasn't thought that part through." Hugh shook his head and rubbed the back of his neck. "I also think her plan is to try and keep her brother from sending troops here." He heaved a heavy sigh and cursed under his breath. "The stubborn fool is willing to put herself in danger to protect everyone else. I must go after her."

"I Cannae let ye go off on yer own. I'll hae Big Alec gather as many men as we can spare and ready at least one wagon as quickly as possible."

Cam rushed away, leaving Hugh alone with his troubling thoughts. He was angry with everyone, but mostly with himself for not paying closer attention to what Freyja had really been saying.

~

The sun had risen some time ago and the morning air was cool. Whereas darkness had loomed heavily in the sky when Freyja fled the castle. Dressed in her knee boots and comfortable men's clothes she favored, she'd snuck out of her room while Hugh lay stretched out over her bed, sound asleep. There wasn't enough time to write him a note explaining her actions, and if she woke him, he definitely wouldn't let her leave. She had no time to argue with the man.

She'd crept out of the room and closed the heavy wood door as quietly as possible. A moment later she caught the scent of fresh bread coming from the kitchen. Silently, she'd made her way across the hall, stepping around people sleeping on straw pallets. She'd followed her nose and crept into the empty kitchen and grabbed a fresh loaf of bread, some dried meat, and filled her pockets with biscuits. Satisfied with her bounty, Freyja slipped out the door, which led to the kitchen garden, and headed for the weapons room. She saw no one standing guard and stepped into the dark room. When her eyes adjusted to the darkness, she'd grabbed a targe, a sghian dubh, then noticed a pile of bedrolls. Tucking a bedroll under her arm, she peeked out the door then ran toward the stables.

"It's all right girl." She patted Saga's neck, flung the rope over the gray mare's neck then made a loop and slipped it around the animal's nose. Concerned about being caught stealing a horse, Freyja immediately saddled the horse and tied on her packs. She led the mare around the back of the stables, remembering the postern gate in the barmekin wall from the day she'd followed little Robbie behind the stables. Due to the early hour, the gate was unguarded.

The hinges creaked as she pushed the large iron gate open. Saga stopped. Her ears twitched, listening for danger, while her eyes searched the area.

"Come, Saga. We have to leave here." Reaching up Freyja straitened the mare's forelock then brushed her hand down over the mare's face. "We have a long ride ahead of us. We have to go." Stepping back, Freyja clicked her tongue, coaxing the mare forward and out through the narrow gate. After closing the gate, she swung up onto Saga's back and trotted away. Once they were a safe distance down the road, she kicked her heels, sending the mare into a gallop.

As she approached the stone hunting lodge, Freyja felt a tightness in her chest but shook it off, and reined Saga to the trail that led down toward the loch. She followed the trail around the east end of the loch and continued northwest toward the coast. Visions of Hugh standing naked in the water and making love to her at his camp, were sure to haunt her throughout her journey home. She would do her best to not dwell on the memories.

She traveled up the hilly terrain that brought her to a forest of dense trees. At first, she enjoyed the scenery and the fact that no one knew where she was. By late afternoon she started to second guess the wisdom in facing her brother alone. Was she foolish enough to think she would actually get a chance to explain to her cousin Duncan and the rest of the clan members what truly happened the day Andrew was murdered?

Would her clan believe her innocence or consider her a fool for risking her life in returning home? Either way, they needed to know the truth of what happened. Whatever they decided to do with the information, she would have to deal with it.

The day grew long, and Freyja was hungry and exhausted. When it became too dark to see the winding trail before her, she stopped for the night. She sat by her campfire chewing on a hunk of tasteless, dried meat. In the quiet, her thoughts returned to Hugh and how peaceful he looked sleeping after they made love. Her chest tightened. She missed him. By now he must be furious with her for leaving without a word or a note. The chance that he might be disappointed in her produced a heavy sadness in her heart, but she needed to reveal the truth to her people and hold Finlay responsible for his evil acts. She hoped Hugh would understand that and one day forgive her.

If Finlay gathered his army and rode to Corell Castle to collect Sorcha, his actions could easily ignite a war between the two clans. If Freyja couldn't stop him, it would be her fault if anyone was hurt or killed.

She pulled the large, waxed cloth tightly around her shoulders, then curled up under a clump of trees just as a light rain started to fall. Her body ached from the cold, and long day in the saddle. Yet, she drifted off to sleep with the sensation of Hugh's strong arms wrapped protectively around her.

~

Hugh was ready to kill someone, anyone. Hours were spent consulting maps to determine the safest route to make the long trip north. They also considered the chances of coming across certain loyalists and English soldiers along the road, and how best to handle them. It was late afternoon when the MacCormac army finally rode through the gates, with several supply and cook wagons following.

As they rode away from Corell Castle, Hugh reckoned the journey through the rough landscape would take Freyja ten to twelve days. One hundred heavily armed men and several wagons would take close to fifteen days. He figured she was a good eight to ten hours ahead of them. A person alone could travel the old Roman roads and trails through forest and valleys a lot faster than an army and wagons could. However, after informing Cam of his wish to set out on his own, Hugh had been ordered to stay with the troops.

He prayed they would catch up to Freyja before she arrived at Dreki Craige Castle. If they didn't, it could possibly be too late to save her.

Eighteen

For most of the day Freyja had followed an old trail along the edge of the forest, wishing to stay dry and out of sight, yet her clothes and boots were wet from the steady rain. She reached into her pocket. She'd made a point of picking up a small pebble each morning to mark the days since she had left Corell Castle. She now had six. It was late afternoon, and her empty stomach grumbled in protest. The food she'd taken from the castle was gone, leaving her with only a small piece of stale bread for her breakfast this morning. She would need to find something to eat soon. The thought of fresh meat, berries, and cool water from a stream gave Freyja the encouragement needed to continue on. She had ridden this way before with her father and knew that tomorrow she faced a steep climb up the side of a mountain. At the top of the ridge, the trail would take her down through the valley and over the moors before it reached the rocky landscape leading to Dreki Craig Castle. Her home.

The trail veered off to the left, leading deeper into the woods. Very little light shown through the canopy, and she realized that soon it would be too dark and difficult for her horse to make her way through the woods. She glanced around looking for a place to camp for the night. She had walked half of the day instead of riding, wanting to save the horse's legs for what lay ahead of them. She hoped exhaustion would help her sleep through the night and keep her from dreaming of Hugh. She missed him so much. His lopsided, boyish grin, and the way his eyes seemed to reveal his thoughts when they were alone. But mostly, she was going to miss the way he stared deeply into her soul, making her heart race, right before he pulled her into his arms and kissed her. And now she'd thrown that all away. Her throat tightened, knowing their relationship was over.

Saga came to a stop, forcing Freyja back from her thoughts. She heard voices further up the trail. From up on the horse's back, she could see a campfire through the trees. Searching the trees for soldiers, she only spotted two men and two women. She wondered how they came to be on this secluded trail. The only village they could have come from was Clachan Craige near Dreki Craige Castle. It was possible that she might know them.

Not wanting to take any chances for a surprise attack, Freyja strapped her targe to her left arm and quietly drew her sword. Slowly, she urged Saga forward, approaching the camp with great caution. Once again, she scanned the area for armed men who might be hiding, waiting for the perfect opportunity to strike. One man chopped wood while the other carried the pieces over to the fire. A woman tended to a large pot set in the coals, as the other woman sat on a log holding a baby in her arms. Freyja counted a total of seven children; the younger ones were playing while the older children constructed pallets for beds. Freyja's vision blurred and she swayed but quickly grabbed the saddle for support.

The man by the fire straightened. When he noticed her approaching their camp, he said something she couldn't hear. Everyone paused what they were doing, turning and staring at her. She must look half-crazed; her hair loose from its braid, her clothes wet and smeared with mud.

The woman with the child stood and turned to face Freyja.

Her eyes squinted as her gaze raked over Freyja's face. Then she smiled and said, "'Tis it really ye, Miss Freyja?" She handed that child over to the other woman and cautiously approached Freyja. "'Tis I, yer friend Kara. Are ye hurt?"

Freyja felt tears on her cheeks. "Kara?" she whispered, suddenly overwhelmed with emotion.

"Aye, miss." The woman smiled and came a little closer. "Freyja, 'tis me, Kara." Freyja stared down at the lass who had been her childhood friend. "Are ye hungry? We have hot food and would be happy to share it with ye."

Freyja's gaze shot to the large pot in the fire then back to Kara. She nodded and placed her sword back into its sheath. "Morgun," the girl called over her shoulder. "Come and see to her horse."

"Please," Kara said, gazing up at Freyja. "Come and eat with us."

Freyja stepped down from the saddle, unsteady and suddenly very vulnerable. Kara helped her remove her targe and handed it to the man she called Morgun. She then took Freyja's hand and led her in the direction of the warm fire and the delicious aroma coming from the huge black pot.

"Please sit." Kara motioned to the log. "I will get ye some food. 'Twill make ye feel better."

"Thank you," she said when Kara handed her a wooden bowl filled with chunks of meat and vegetables covered in a thick broth.

"I hate to take your food; accept it smells delicious." She smiled at Kara while the older woman filled bowls for the children. The first spoonful tasted heavenly and instantly revived Freyja.

The young boy across from Freyja scrunched up his nose and whispered, "She looks as if she hasnae eaten in days." The older woman shushed him and told him to eat his supper.

"Oh Freyja," Kara said, sitting down alongside of her on the log. "'Tis good to see ye. Though, 'tis like seeing a ghost as we all thought ye were dead." She wrung her hands together and added. "I dinnae think I would ever see ye again." Kara placed her hand on Freyja's arm. "Freyja, are ye heading to Dreki Craige Castle? Are ye planning to face yer brother?"

Freyja wiped her sleeve across her face and stood. "Thank you for your kindness."

Kara jumped to her feet. "Freyja, ye cannae stand up to him alone. Everyone knows yer not a killer. Ye know not what yer brother and his men hae done since ye've been gone." Freyja handed her the empty bowl. She was tired and had several long hard hours ahead of her tomorrow. She was not up to arguing with Kara.

Kara took Freyja's hands and clutched them to her breast. The girl's eyes displayed her anxiety. "There is no one supervising the men. No one seeing to the work and the fields hae not been planted. Young boys hae been beaten and several girls raped. Yer brother and his men do what they like without fear of any consequences."

Freyja drew in a deep breath and exhaled slowly as she squeezed Kare's trembling hands. She had witnessed her brother's wickedness and had expected that it would not stop. "What of Duncan," she asked. She would kill Finlay if her sweet cousin, Duncan had been harmed in her absence. "Do you know if he is well?"

"I donae know." The girl shook her head and released Freyja's hands. "What is happening has driven not only our family but many others away from their homes to seek out new places and new clans."

Folding her arms over her chest to keep anyone from seeing them tremble, Freyja turned toward the fire. Heat rose to her face, not from the flames, but from anger and disdain for Finlay. He had killed Andrew and possibly ordered her death. And to what gain? He was letting the clan fall into ruin and his men run uncontrolled. He was no laird. "This is another reason why I must go back and set thing right." Was she strong enough physically and mentally to defeat Finlay and take over as Laird and Chieftain of Clan Weir?

~

For nine days, Hugh had been traveling from Corell Castle with Cam, Big Alec, and a hundred well-armed soldiers, and the sluggish progress was beginning to wear on his nerves.

The first three days it rained constantly. The old Roman road they had chosen to travel was covered in mud, making their journey more challenging.

Scouts had been sent out on numerous trails in search of Freyja. The first couple of scout came back and reported they hadn't seen any signs of her or where she had camped. When the last rider returned with the same message, Hugh cursed under his breath. Hunching his shoulders against the miserable wind and rain, he pulled his plaid up and over his head.

He was sure Freyja had headed towards her home, but without any trace of her tracks, it would make catching her before she reached Dreki Craige Castle impossible.

"Are ye sure ye cannae live without this lass?" Cam asked Hugh as they rode along.

Hugh stared at his cousin sitting on the horse next to him. "Aye. I weel get her back."

Cam stared at him and asked, "Then what are ye so upset aboot? Ye've been in worse circumstances than this afore."

"Aye," Hugh snarled, ready to release his anger on whoever was the closest. "Like the week we sat in a cell at Fort Inverlocky waiting to be hanged, because ye dinnae hae sense enough to realize ye were in love with yer wife, so ye sent the poor lass away?" Hugh shook his head and grumbled under his breath, "Eeejit."

"Poor lass?" Cam turned to Big Alec and said, "Alec, knock

him out and throw him into the back of one of the wagons. He can ride for the rest of the trip there. When Big Alec grinned, Cam chuckled, then added, "I wouldnae consider Lady Adriana a, *poor lass.*"

"Aye." Hugh laughed. "She stood up to Colonel Robert Stone and arranged for our release."

"I recall my Lady wife also stood up to ye." Cam smirked at Hugh.

"Oh, aye." Hugh nodded. "Ye mean the night she and sweet Bethany drugged yer brandy, knocking ye out cold, so she could seduce ye, yet again?"

Although he chuckled, Cam frowned and replied, "We weel no be speaking of that night ever again."

Hugh leaned forward and glanced around Cam to Big Alec and mouthed, "'Twas two nights."

"Shut yer gob ye dobber," Cam quickly added.

Big Alec tilted back his head and roared with laughter then said, "My sweet little, harmless, Bethany. Did ye know one night, in the dark I snuck into the buttery to snatch some biscuits, and I happened upon Bethany. I scared the lass so badly, that she grabbed a long metal stirring spoon and beat me with it as she chased me into the Great Hall." He shook his head. "I was terrified a pack of demons were after me and going to kill me." They all laughed, and Alec added, "The wee lass still scares me. *All* lasses scare me."

Their laughter died down, and they continued riding in silence. Despite the lighthearted conversation, there was a huge hollowness in Hugh's chest. Freyja was to be his wife and the mother of his children. They were to be a family. He still wants that, but none of that could happen if her brother got the chance to finish what he'd started.

Big Alec had managed to maneuver his horse between Hugh's and Cam's. In a low voice he said, "She'll be fine, laddie. 'Tis time she has faith in herself. She needs to believe she is a true warrior. That she's brave and strong enough to be Laird and

Chieftain. By showing up and confronting her brother, she will gain her clans respect, and they will listen to her."

Hugh glanced over at Alec. "Aye, if she lives long enough." Alec nodded then turned and spoke to Cam. The thought of not reaching Freyja in time made Hugh's stomach roll and a sour taste rise to the back of his throat. He swiped the back of his hand across his sweaty brow. His future depended on his ability to catch-up to her in time.

A sense a panic washed over Hugh, and he felt it hard to breathe.

"Cam," Hugh hollered. "We are moving too slow. I'm going on ahead."

Hugh didn't pay attention to what Cam said to Big Alec, but the big warrior fell back. Soon he reappeared on Cam's left side, and twenty mounted soldiers fell in line behind them.

Cam gave a nod, and the group broke into a gallop.

Hugh's only thought was that he couldn't lose Freyja, couldn't live without her.

The scent of sea salt carried on the breeze reached Freyja. She paused as the path opened up from the woods, revealing Dreki Craige Castle's crenellated tower adorned with green, black, and gold flags. Built by her Norse and Celtic ancestors, the castle was constructed from black stone quarried from the nearby cliffs. Freyja admired the remarkable craftsmanship displayed in the ancient fortress and the numerous stone dragons and sea serpents carved into the dark walls and perched atop the battlements. Towering above the coastline, the fortress appeared both formidable and menacing from all angles.

When she came into view of the guards, revealing her presence, horns sounded announcing her arrival. If she persisted, this could be the end for her. Her stomach twisted at the thought of never seeing the huge colorful tapestries and the beautifully carved furniture, within the castle that her great-grandfather had commissioned from Europe over a hundred years ago.

She'd questioned her sanity throughout the trip, but last evening her doubt was particularly acute. However, after a hot meal and a peaceful night's sleep, and what she had learned from Kara, she knew what had to be done, and she wouldn't fail Andrew or her clan.

Freyja stopped some distance from the closed gates and called to the guard, "I demand to address my brother, Larid Finlay Weir, and his second, my cousin, Duncan Weir."

After a moment the guard replied, "His Lordship has been summoned."

Saga danced in place and then turned in a wide circle.

Then he appeared, a ghostly vision with Andrew's white fox cape draped over his shoulders. He stared down at her from the safety of the battlement. "I did not believe my ears when I was told 'twas you demanding my attention. Do I need to remind you, Freyja that you are not welcome here?"

"I want not from you, Brother," She yelled. "I only wish for the clan to know the truth of why your goons took me away from here."

"Everyone here knows the truth of what you did, Sister."

"They know only the lies you have told them, Finlay. They deserve to know the real truth."

"You dare to call me a liar?" Finlay's voice rose to a near screech.

"You accused me of killing Andrew. Yes, I call you a liar."

"You forget, Freyja that I rule Dreki Craige Castle now and the Weir Clan. My word is the law."

Saga spun in another circle. "From the clan members who have left you, which I met on the road, there *is* no law here. They say you and your men do as you wish with no regard for anyone else."

"Now you challenge my rule?" He raised his arm toward the sky and shook his fist.

She had broken open a beehive. The sharp stings would surely follow. Saga stomped her hoof then reared and tossed her head. Freyja turned the mare back toward the wall and yelled, "Do you think you are brave enough to go up against someone who can fight back? Someone who's not ill and close to death?"

Finlay stared down at her; his face flushed with rage. He waved his arms in the air and the clanking of the iron gates being unlocked and pulled open could be heard. A moment later a warrior on the back of his great destroyer emerged and rode out over the drawbridge.

Saga pranced in place as if anticipating the imminent battle. "Easy Saga," she whispered. The rider held his targe and reins in his left hand; in his right he clutched his sword. He approached her slowly.

"That won't be a problem, baby sister," her brother called down, using the endearment he knew she despised, then laughed. Freyja never took her eyes off the rider. As he drew closer, she realized it was Torcall. His grin exposed his brown, broken teeth. He was going to kill her. Freyja quickly untied her targe and slipped her left arm through the leather straps and drew her sword. Saga stomped her hoof and snorted.

"Ye should hae stayed dead, Freyja," Torcall taunted, as he drew closer. He swung his sword over and around his horse's head. Freyja positioned her leg back towards Saga's flank instructing the mare to move only her hips and back legs around, so they remained facing her attacker.

Torcall's horse charged forward as if to ram into Freyja, but Saga sidestepped. Freyja brought her sword down hitting Torcall's with a loud clang and following through as he passed. Swinging her horse around, Freyja kept her sword low, and when Torcall approached she swung her sword and nicked his leg.

He cursed, urged his horse forward and swung his sword.

She blocked the strike with her targe. Their swords clashed repeatedly, the sound was deafening. They were equally matched. Sweat rolled down Freyja's back and chest. Torcall rammed his horse into hers, their swords locked, and they struggled. He gave a mighty shove, and Freyja hit the ground. Pain shot up her spine and spots flashed before her eyes. From somewhere she heard a voice yelling for her to get up. She struggled to her feet.

There was a low growl behind her. Freyja turned in time to block Torcall's attack. Their swords clanged together, steel rasped as it slid across steel. With every strike Freyja deflected, she relived the beating Torcall gave her that day in the woods. Sweat burned her eyes as it dripped down her face. Her chest expanded deeply with every breath and her heart thumped in her ears. They circled each other. Every blow and trust he perpetrated only motivated Freyja's determination to defeat him.

A group of soldiers had gathered around them; their eyes filled with concern as they watched. Freyja advanced, pushing Torcall back. Anger raged in his eyes, and he frantically swung and sliced his sword at her. She deflected his attacks with her sword and targe.

Exhausted, Freyja retreated a few steps. Torcall growled and advanced with murder in his eyes. Suddenly, Freyja was seized from behind. Her upper arms secured by two soldiers. Duncan Weir, her younger cousin, stepped in front of Freyja and took her sword. She couldn't believe he had betrayed her.

Torcall roared in protest as he came forward. Duncan turned his back on Freyja. He raised his hand to stop the man and said in a loud voice, "This is done for today, Torcall." He turned back to the soldiers who held her captive and added, "Take her and secure her in the dungeon."

Freyja stood tall. She wouldn't allow herself to crumble before her people. "Duncan," she said as he passed her. "My horse? I ask she be taken care of. Saga is a warrior's horse and should be treated as one." He replied with only a slight nod, then walked away.

Men crowded around her. Still supported by the two men, she was led through the cold stone tunnels, to the dungeon, deep in the bowels of the castle. The soldiers' low voices mingled together, and she was unable to discern what they said. Her thoughts still questioned why her dear cousin, Duncan, had betrayed her.

Nineteen

The old Roman road led them to the northwest corner of Scotland and Freyja's home. Horns sounded their arrival long before the ominous castle appeared on the horizon. Giant flags waved the Weir colors from the four corners of the huge tower house. Dreki Craige Castle was suitably named, Hugh thought as he spotted several stone sea serpents and dragons guarding the tower, stone sentinels, seemingly waiting for the signal to attack their enemies.

Hugh's fascination with mythology reminded him that "Dreki" was the Norse word for dragons and sea serpents, and "Craige" was a Gaelic word for rocky cliffs. The stronghold reflected her heritage and the castle's location.

Spying several other serpents and dragons sprawled across the stone walls of the tower house, Hugh wished he was traveling here with Freyja, learning more about her family's background, and the ancestors who had built this enthralling fortress. Instead, he rode ready for whatever obstacles may arise in retrieving her from her brother's castle.

Hugh, Cam, Big Alec, and twenty soldiers rode toward the closed gates and the soldiers positioned safely behind it. Fifty or more soldiers lined the battlement.

"It would seem they were expecting us," Cam stated as his horse stopped next to Hugh's.

A moment later, Laird Finlay Weir came into view on the battlement. Hugh snickered under his breath, for the young laird was once again, dressed to impress. Weir seemed fond of wearing his blond wig and black Tricorne hat with one long ostrich feather.

Hugh had a strong urge to call out the pompous young laird, but instead he glanced over to Cam, silently requesting his Laird's permission to proceed. Cam answered with a nod and a forewarned look, slightly reminding Hugh that they were not there to start a conflict; though they were ready if Weir challenged them. Hugh nudged his big bay forward. "Hugh Robertson MacCormac, milord. I request an audience with yer sister, Miss Freyja Weir."

"I am sorry, old man." Finlay frowned feigning sympathy and added, "But I am afraid my dear little sister does not wish to see or speak with you."

The man was lying; Freyja would never say such a thing. "I willnae leave until I see Freyja and hear her wishes from her own lips," Hugh roared as he yelled up at Weir.

Cam whispered, "Easy noo. Donae be losing yer heid."

Hugh drew in and exhaled short breaths, his lips pinched together tightly. He needed to see for himself that Freyja was unharmed. He didn't know what he would do if Weir didn't produce her soon.

Laird Finlay tilted his head and spoke to someone, then waved the man away. He turned back to Hugh, then gazed out over the other mounted soldiers. "Stay where you are. I have sent my man for her. Even so, pray you are not too disappointed by her words, MacCormac. You know how fickle women can sometimes be," he replied, shaking his head several times.

Hugh nodded once and quietly returned to his position next to Cam. He feared any response from him might surpass the arrogant man's sardonic tone and that would hinder their intentions.

Several moments passed and Freyja had not appeared. "What is taking so long," he said, his voice just above a murmur. "Something is wrong. If she's hurt, someone will answer to the end of my sword."

"Easy mon." He heard Cam's deep voice beside him. "Show some patience. This is a game to Weir, like the game of chess. Any move ye make noo shall affect the outcome of the match. Weir's ego will press him to make poor decisions, and he'll lose the game in the end."

Finally, Freyja appeared beside her brother on the battlement. Her face pale as the clouds in the sky. She leaned forward between the crenels and called down, "What are you are doing, Hugh?" Her gaze moved from Hugh to Cam, and to the small army of men behind them. "You should not have come here," she stated. "Please take your men and go."

Hugh's gaze stayed on Freyja, desperately searching for any sign of her true feelings, but the distance made it impossible to read her expression. Did she really not want him here?

"May I speak with ye in private, Miss Freyja?"

Freyja slowly shook her head and said, "No. It would be best for everyone if you would leave at once." Finlay whispered to her then slipped his arm around her shoulder.

Every muscle in Hugh's contracted as he watched the same hands Weir used to smother his own brother rest possessively on Freyja's shoulders.

He turned to Cam and noticed that the other eighty soldiers had shown up and had formed a line behind them, ready to fight if given the command.

His gaze shot up to her when she said, "Everything is all right. My place in here, and my duty is to my brother and my clan." Her voice seemed agitated. She glanced away, then back and added, "I've had many days to search my heart and soul, and

I have found that I no longer wish to marry you. Hugh... I am so sorry for all of this."

Hugh's chest constricted with a stabbing pain at Freyja's words. Crushed and utterly defeated, he couldn't speak. He could barely move. Silence hung heavily on the salty air. Logic told him she belonged with her family and clan. His heart wanted her for himself. What he was supposed to do now.

"Laird Weir," Cam bellowed as his horse stepped forward. "We thank ye for granting us the opportunity to speak with Miss Freyja. We shall honor her wishes and depart." He offered a quick nod.

Weir's eyes squinted and he grinned. "You are a wise man, Laird MacCormac. I am truly sorry my sister has rejected your man, but we are delighted to have her back here with us again. Alive and well." Finley squeezed Freyja to his side. "Do have a safe journey back home, and inform Miss Sorcha Sinclair, I shall arrive very soon to collect her." His statement may have been ignored, but it hadn't gone unnoticed.

Big Alec growled and nudged his horse forward.

Cam's mount moved next, yet Hugh couldn't make himself abandon Freyja into her brother's arms. Even as the line of soldiers began to shift, Hugh lingered, his heart aching for the woman who now seemed lost to him. The sight of Freyja looking subservient to her brother, so unlike her true self, made Hugh's blood boil, but hearing her proclaim her loyalty to her clan changed things. His resolve faltered and a silent war raged between duty and longing.

He continued to stare up at her for a few more seconds. This wasn't right. She must still love him, but she was sending him away. He turned his horse in front of Cam, forcing his cousin to stop. "I concede yer are my Laird, but ye are wrong in this. We cannae leave without fighting for her. Yer know what he's capable of doing. We cannae leave her here."

"Hugh," Cam interrupted, "Noo 'tis not the time for action. There are still chessmen on the board. This game of his 'tis not over yet. Besides, if he wanted to kill her, he's had plenty of time to do so. Come noo, we must leave."

Hugh turned, solemnly, and followed Cam and Alec away from Dreki Craige Castle and his beloved Freyja.

~

Freyja couldn't hold back the tears any longer, as Finlay forced her to stand next to him on the battlement and watch Hugh and the rest of the MacCormac soldiers ride away. It had broken her heart to lie to him and send him away, but she had done what she needed to do. She wouldn't blame him if he hated her, she in fact loathed herself at the moment for getting into this horrible situation.

"Take her below and lock her back up." Finlay roared, pushing her toward one of his men.

"Finlay, I did what you asked, so let me go."

"Ha, so you can ride after them and bring the whole MacCormac and Sinclair clans down on me? I think not, little sister."

Freyja tried to reason with her brother but was not heard. Two soldiers quickly dragged her back down into the dungeon. They shoved her into the cell and when the iron door locked, her heart sank.

She sat down on the thin straw pallet and leaned up against the stone wall. Finlay's whispered threat replayed in her mind: "If you don't say exactly what I tell you, Torcall will cut Duncan's throat." The image of Torcall standing next to Duncan, knowing he could kill him at any moment, would not go away. His words would haunt her for the rest of her life, however long that would be. Her life might end sooner than she'd imagined.

Freyja wondered if Duncan had any idea why he had been brought up onto the battlement, or that his life had even been in danger. Was he safe now?

What would happen next? Hugh had been her only hope of surviving. She took a ragged breath and let it out slowly. Would they hang her or leave her to die alone in this cold, damp cell.

There were no windows to tell the time of day or day from night. She slid sideways down the wall and once she landed on the thin layer of straw that separated her from the stone floor, she curled up on her side. She would not weep. This was her punishment for assuming that honesty would expose Finlay's malicious plans, and that the goodness of her people would help hold him accountable. Finally, after what seemed like endless hours, fatigue overtook her, and she slipped into a restless slumber. Images of Hugh's face marred by hurt and confusion—as he grappled with the pain of her sending him away without an explanation, drifted through her dreams.

The hours dragged on for Freyja while she was held captive. Finally, after two long days, three soldiers Freyja didn't recognize entered the dungeon. She stood back from the bars and studied them warily as they approached her cell. "What is happening?" she asked as one of the soldiers unlocked the cell door, stepped inside, and ushered her toward the opening. "Where are you taking me?" She glanced from one man to the other. "Tell me what's going on."

The third man standing outside the cell announced, in a voice that sounded overly loud to Freyja, "The clan council has been in session since this morning. We were ordered to bring ye up."

This was it. Her hands shook as she reached out and placed her hand on the stone wall for support. There was only one reason for her to be summoned by the clan council. She sighed, anticipating being given another fake trial and this time... Finlay would have her put to death. A lump formed in her throat and her eyes welled up with tears, but Freyja wouldn't let her fear and sorrow show. She straightened her shoulders, lifted her chin, and walked bravely out of her cell. If she was to meet her death, she would not go as a coward. She followed the soldiers up the stone stairs to where her fate awaited.

Freyja's mind was in a haze, revealing events and people from her past. She remembered things she hadn't thought about in years, like her fifth birthday and her father, Lochlan Weir, giving her a white pony. When they rode together, he told her storied about the history of their clan, and how important it was for the laird and chieftain to protect and provide for their people.

She thought of her mother, Marie, who was kind, loving, strong, and compassionate. She was tall and willowy, with reddish-blond hair and green eyes. Even after all these years since her death, Freyja still missed her mother—every day. But it wouldn't be long, and she would be reunited with her father, mother, and Andrew once again.

"In here, Miss," the guard said, opening the door to a small chamber next to the chieftain's hall. Freyja could hear muffled voices. She hadn't been in this space in years. When she was young, she would hide here from her brothers. They never found her. Looking back on it now, maybe they had never even tried to find her. Once the door was closed and locked, she sank down onto a chair and wondered what had changed Finlay into the ruthless person he was now.

"Oh, Hugh," she whispered, "if you only knew, I had no choice but to send you away. If not for my lies, poor Duncan would have been killed." Tears rolled down her cheeks, and she prayed her sacrifices were not made in vain and that Duncan still lived. Her thoughts returned to Hugh, and her anger rose as she wondered why he hadn't argued or even tried to fight for her. It seemed like it had been easy for him to give up on them, their love, and their future. He had simply ridden away without looking back. No matter how much she loved Hugh and wanted to be with him, it was over. She would never get the chance to tell him the truth and explain why she lied to him. Freyja told herself to stay strong and be brave. Now, who was she lying to, she thought as her trembling hands wiped away her tears.

Freyja turned to face the door as it was unlocked and swung open. Her cousin Duncan hurried in. "Oh, Duncan." She threw her arms around his neck. "I am so glad to see you. I worried that Torcall might have killed you."

Duncan pushed her away and handed her a sword. "We must hurry, Freyja. We haven't much time. Yer brother and his men are gathered together in the Chieftain's Hall waiting for ye."

Freyja felt lightheaded as she listened to what he was saying and fastened the belt around her waist. "Duncan, I don't understand. What's going on?"

"There's no time to talk, we are taking over. The majority of the clan support ye as our new laird."

"What?" She stared at him in disbelief. He couldn't be serious. She could never overthrow her brother.

Duncan grabbed her by the arm and dragged her toward the door. "Ye hae proven to the clan that ye are brave and shrewd. Ye will make a great leader." When he opened the door, he put a finger to his mouth, indicating for her to be silent. Freyja nodded but still didn't understand exactly what her cousin had expected from her. When she stepped out, she paused. There was a mixture of soldiers, villagers, and an array of castle folk lined up in the corridor as far as she could see.

Duncan stepped forward in front of the large crowd and turned to face her. He placed his right fist over his heart. Freyja drew in a deep breath as everyone behind him quietly did the same. "Freyja Weir of Clachan Craige," he said solemnly. "We who stand afore ye swear our loyalty to ye and accept ye as our Laird and Chieftain." Duncan bowed his head as did everyone else in a long silent wave.

"Yer brother and his men are all together in one place," he whispered, "We have the element of surprise. 'Tis ye or him.

One of ye will die this day. The other will rule over Clachan Craige and Clan Weir."

Placing her hand on the hilt of her sword, Freyja gave Duncan a nod. Duncan glanced around her, and she turned to see the guard posted at the entrance to the hall, nod to Duncan. "'Tis set. The rest are in place and ready my laird."

Freyja drew in a deep breath and prayed that the great Lairds before her would give her strength and wisdom to see this done. Filled with a conviction she hadn't known she possessed; Freyja walked toward the entrance and strolled confidently into the chieftain's hall.

She met and held Finlay's stare as she crossed the room and stood before him. She raised her chin and fingered the hilt of her sword in anticipation of a fight. Finlay sneered back at her. Torcall jumped to his feet. His chair flew backwards, and he drew his sword.

Freyja held her brother's stare, daring him to break the contact first. Behind her, she heard the raspy sound of swords being pulled from their leather sheaths. Finlay squinted at her, his face flushed as he suddenly understood what was taking place.

"It would seem you have caught me unawares, little sister. Yet, I don't understand how you think you will get away with your display of treason," he said, slowly rising to his feet before her.

Freyja felt a sudden calm wash over her and felt her lips rise in lopsided grin. "It would appear that I already have." Finlay's nostrils flared and he frowned. "I, Freyja Weir of Clachan Craige, accuse these men of corruption and acts of violence against the clan. As for you, Finlay Weir, I accuse you of grave incompetence and the murder of your own brother, Laird Andrew Weir."

Finlay slammed his hand down on the table and spat, "Who do you think you are to dare to speak to me in this manner?"

"As the new Laird and Chieftain of Dreki Craige Castle and

Clan Weir, and the village of Clachan Craige, I order you and these men by taken up to the parapet and thrown into the sea, as our ancestors dealt with criminals."

"I should have killed you myself when I had the chance." Finlay held eye contact with her while he was seized, disarmed, and his wrists shackled together.

Freyja's body was rigid, like a stone statue, unable to move until all of the men were led out through the door that led to the top of the keep.

"My laird," Duncan spoke softly beside her. He'd appeared without her seeing or hearing him. "Are ye all right, Freyja?" he whispered. She turned and looked at him. "Breathe. Ye did good. Just breathe."

She smiled and uttered, "And always watch your flank."

~

Twelve days later, the weary and despondent men rode through the gates of Corell Castle. Hugh dismounted, groaning when his feet hit the hard ground. His cousin's solemn voice drifted to him on the cool, afternoon breeze. "Ye are expected in the Great Hall this evening for supper." When Hugh shook his head and was about to decline, Cam shot him a cautionary glare and said, "'Tis not an invitation. 'Tis an order."

A stable boy appeared to take Perseus. Handing over the reins, Hugh said, "Rub him down good lad, and put him out on grass. I'll see to his feed later." When Hugh turned to speak with Cam, his cousin had already entered the inner bailey. Hugh rolled his stiff and sore shoulders. He needed several mugs of ale to rid his mind of the image of Freyja, standing on the battlement telling him to leave. He released a sigh and thought an hour or two in a deep tub of boiling water would help relieve his physical aches. But what of the ache in his chest?

~

The din in the Great Hall fell silent when Hugh crossed the threshold. By everyone's expressions, they all knew Freyja had rejected him and sent him away. That news combined with Finlay's announcement that he would soon come for Sorcha, caused fear of an attack to spread quickly throughout the MacCormac Clan.

Hugh stepped up onto the dais and took his place next to Cam, flinging his long, wet hair over his shoulder. He'd see Maddy later and ask her to cut half of it off. He blinked at the food placed before him. He'd fallen asleep in his bath after drinking enough ale, that one or two more would likely put him on his bum for the rest of the night.

Hugh ate in silence, while Cam kept anyone from approaching him. Once he'd finished eating, Hugh glanced up and caught Maddy watching him. The sweet old lass discreetly pointed one finger toward the rafters, signaling him to wait. She then turned and then slipped down the back steps toward the kitchen. Moments later, she reappeared holding a small bundle. Smiling at Hugh, she tilted her head toward the south entrance and hurried off in that direction. Discreetly, he stood and stepped off the platform and followed her.

Maddy's round cheeks were bright pink as she smiled at him. She handed him the bundle. "Here noo," she whispered. "Take this and go tend to yer wounds, laddie. But donae be given up on that lass. I hae seen how she looks at ye. 'Tis the same way ye look at her."

Hugh leaned over and kissed the old woman's cheek. "Thanks lassie. 'Tis a wonder I could ever have eyes for another woman with the way you've spoiled me."

"Go on noo. But mind ye behave and stay safe."

"I will, love." He gazed affectionately at the woman who had cared for him like a mother ever since his own had died.

"And donae be gone long." She reached up and patted his cheek with her hand. "Noo, off wi' ye, ye rascal!". Hugh kissed her forehead, turned and headed down the corridor.

Normally, he had approached every situation logically, whether evaluating the best strategy for an attack or choosing a piece of meat from a trencher. Nevertheless, at the moment, it seemed his logical mind had deserted him, and his rational thinking was no longer present. As he ambled across the bailey, he passed several people who either tried to comfort him or asked him questions concerning Freyja or Sorcha. He longed to be left alone; afraid he might take his pain and his mounting frustration out on some unexpecting soul.

Hugh entered his chambers and gathered a few of his belongings. A few moments later he rode out the main gate. It wouldn't take long before the news of him leaving was delivered to Cam, but he didn't care. He needed to be alone for a while.

Within an hour, Hugh recognized the men's voices as they neared the hunting lodge. The door opened and Cam and Malcolm strolled in. They each held a bottle of Cam's best brandy. "What took ye so long," Hugh asked as they set the bottles down on the table.

"When you left the hall and didn't come back, we figured we'd find ye here," Malcolm stated calmly.

Cam slid a chair out from the table and sat down. "After ye left," Cam said. "Auntie Moira declared 'tis time ye and Sorcha were married afore Laird Weir, and his army shows up and attempts to take her."

"Aye." Malcolm walked over to the open cupboard and returned with three cups. "We had to get away from the castle. She's turning the whole place upside down with preparations for yer wedding."

"Ye cannae be serious?" Hugh glanced from one man to the other. "I'll no be marrying Sorcha Sinclair."

"Aye, she's serious, mon," Malcolm added as he filled the

cups. "She was ordering people to make extra candles, and to polish the silver and the brass, and all the crystal."

Hugh swallowed his drink in one gulp.

"'Tis a mess," Cam said, shaking his head. "Ye'd think she and the maids were getting ready for Hogmanay."

"Just when is this to take place?" Hugh's stomach twisting into knots as he imagined Sorcha as his wife.

"Here," Malcolm poured more brandy into Hugh's glass. "The wedding is to take place day after tomorrow. Miss Sorcha needs to be wedded, bedded, and fully protected by the MacCormac's as soon as possible."

Cam raised one bushy black eyebrow. "We're here to fetch ye back. We need to prepare for Weir's inevitable arrival and whatever plans he has to claim Sorcha."

Hugh finished his drink and set the cup down. Leaning forward on his elbows, he buried his face in his hands and pushed his fingers through his hair. His duty to protect and keep his clan safe was crucial, but at what cost.

Twenty

Hugh stood like a statue before the people gathered together in the small church at Corell Castle. Father Fitzgerald, the feeble looking, gray-haired priest, stood next to him, mumbling to himself. It has been two days since he sat with his two cousins and drank the night away. He'd come away from that night reminded that duty to clan came before all else. Since Freya had rejected him, it didn't matter what his individual wants may be, he swore he would do whatever was necessary to spare the lives of his distant cousin Sorcha, and their two clans. He must marry her. It was the only way to protect her; besides it was his responsibility as second-in-command. Weir could launch an assault on Corell Castle, but he could never claim Sorcha since she would already be married to Hugh. Furthermore, his troops wouldn't just face the MacCormac warriors; they'd also have to contend with the massive army led by Laird Robert Sinclair.

Hugh maintained his composure, although he would rather be anywhere else. He focused on the large double doors at the back of the church and avoided making eye contact with anyone. It wasn't easy for him to stand there knowing it would be Sorcha walking down the aisle toward him and not Freyja. The overwhelming odor of the dozens of candles burning turned his stomach and he almost retched. This was to be his future.

Sorcha entered the kirk, dressed in a light yellow gown; her black hair covered by a lacy yellow kertch. Her expression was guarded, and Hugh couldn't tell if she was delighted to be marrying him or just as despondent about this marriage as he was? They barely knew one another. They hadn't spent much time together to talk, but he figured there would be plenty of time for that later. They would soon be joined before family, friends, and God, for the rest of their lives.

She started down the aisle toward him. With her tiny curveless frame, she looked like a child of twelve. An image of Freyja, naked upon his bed, her luscious curves exposed to him to enjoy, invaded his mind. His body ached to hold her in his arms again. Why hadn't he stayed and tried to convince her to speak with him in private? Pride. His stupid pride. When someone rejects you, you don't beg them to love you. You walk away. And Freyja had rejected him in no uncertain terms.

As Sorcha drew closer, panic washed over Hugh. He started to sweat, despite the damp chill in the air that hung heavy in the old stone kirk. This was not what he wanted, yet Freyja had made it clear that *he* hadn't been what *she* had wanted. Marrying Sorcha was his duty to his clan, and Hugh had never taken his responsibilities lightly in the past. He wasn't about to start now.

Sorcha finally reached the front of the crowded church. Father Fitzgerald opened his ancient bible. His voice thundered in the silence, which caused Hugh to flinch as he started the ceremony. He stared down at his bride-to-be, trying to listen to and understand the priest's sacred words, but they sounded jumbled to Hugh's ears. Sorcha turned to Lynette and handed her the boutique of flowers she'd been holding.

How long had Lynette been standing next to Sorcha? Hugh turned to the side and found Malcolm standing next to him and wondered just how long he had been there.

Sorcha reached out for Hugh's hands, but before he could

take her hands in his, the double doors at the back of the church crashed open. Hugh turned and saw Freyja march in. Murmurs filled the church as everyone turned to see what was happening.

Dressed and armed as a warrior and chief, Freyja, followed by ten warriors marched up the aisle. What was she up to, now? Instinctively, his fists went to rest on his hips. Where the hell was his sword? Had this all been a rouse? Was she here to start a war on her brother's behalf? Had this all been just a game.

Freyja stopped in front of Hugh and Sorcha. Ignoring everyone else in the church, she turned to face Sorcha and stated, "Miss Sorcha Sinclair, I have come to notify you of the death of your betrothed, Laird Finlay Weir, and to inform you that you are relieved of any obligations you may have had with him. But I see that you already have intentions to marry another."

A wide grin crossed Sorcha's face and glanced up at Hugh. Swallowing hard, she asked, "Hugh do ye love me with all yer heart and soul?"

Staring down at her, Hugh cleared his throat and said, "Nay lass. I am sorry but I do not love ye, at least not romantically, Cousin."

Tears welled up in the girl's eyes as she smiled up at him. "Nor do I love ye." She glanced at Freyja with a smug expression then back to Hugh and added, "Ye are relieved of yer promise to marry me. My champion, Hugh MacCormac."

Hugh smiled. Taking Sorcha's hands in his, he raised them to his lips and placed a light kiss upon her knuckles.

Sorcha's gaze went from Hugh to Freyja, and she whispered, "Thank you." Lifting her skirts, Sorcha raised her chin and strolled back down the aisle alone, and out the doors.

Freyja drew her attention back to Hugh. His tight fists were once again on his hips, his posture almost stone-like, and a stern expression on his face. "We need to talk," she said. "Get a few things straightened out between us." Chuckles and snickers from the church members followed her statement. Freyja's gaze drifted over the members who appeared quite content to stay in their seats and see what would happen next. She spotted Lady Adriana and Bethany sitting next to each other, both were smiling and nodding their heads.

"What do ye think yer doing?" Hugh growled, drawing Freyja's attention back to him. "How did ye get in here, anyways?" He shot a look to the guards standing just outside of the large wooden doors.

Freyja mocked him, by placing her hands on her hips and straightening to her full height. "When I arrived and asked to speak with you, I was informed you were getting married." She felt her face harden, her teeth clenched tightly together as she stared back at him. "Once I got to the chapel, I was forbidden to enter until the ceremony was over." She inhaled sharply, and said, "In spite of this, I revealed my sword and informed the guards if they wished to keep their heads, it would be wise to get out of my way."

He peered past her to the warriors still standing at the entrance. "Hae ye traveled all this way with merely ten men?"

"There are a hundred and fifty more soldiers camped beyond the barmekin wall. I did not see the need to bring more than ten with me when I entered the outer bailey."

Hugh shot her a look and exhaled loudly. But before he could speak Freyja asked in a stern voice, "Are there any more questions you'd like to ask me before we move ahead to more important information I have come to share?"

Hugh's thick brows furrowed over his amber eyes, and his full lips tightened into a thin line. He leaned slightly forward, ready for an argument, even if they were in church. "Did you say Laird Weir is dead?"

"The day you arrived at Dreki Craige Castle, Finlay sent two guards to fetch me from the dungeon, where I'd been held for several days, and brought me up onto the battlement. My cousin Duncan, whom I love dearly, stood next to Torcall. Finlay informed me if I did not repeat his words as he told them to me,

Torcall would slit Duncan's throat. Knowing Finlay, I had no doubt he would carry out the threat."

She saw the muscles in Hugh's jaws bulge and his nostrils flare. "So, you see, I had to tell you I didn't want to see you and not to ever come back." A deafening silence filled the small kirk as she waited for Hugh to respond. Relief washed over Freyja when she saw Hugh's handsome face soften and his eyes fill with compassion. She relaxed and let out a sigh.

Hugh stepped forward, gently taking Freyja's hands in his. In a deep, sincere voice he admitted, "Freyja, I love ye. I want ye to know, I would have torn that castle down piece by piece that day to get to ye, if I had one inkling ye still wanted me." A soft smile played at the corner of his lips. "I give ye my word that no matter where ye are lass, I will come after ye, and I will follow ye wherever ye go."

"'Tis a good thing, Hugh Robertson MacCormac." She smiled. "For I am here to offer you a partnership in ruling Dreki Craige Castle, Clan Weir, and all its holdings with me." Before he could question her, Freyja squeezed his hands and added, "I love you, too. I want you to come back with me and rule beside me as my husband?"

Hugh hesitated for a second. "Lass, are ye asking me to marry ye?"

"Aye, I guess I am," she answered with a grin.

He chuckled, then pulled her into his arms. He kissed her softly at first, but soon the kiss grew more passionate. However, the joyful cheers from their family and friends, and a tap on the shoulder from Malcolm, reminded him where they were. Their reunion would have to wait until later when they could be alone.

~

The week Freyja and Hugh arrived at Dreki Craige Castle, was busy with preparations for the Weir Clan Gathering and Freyja and Hugh's wedding celebration. Each day more clan members and guests arrived. Once all the rooms in the castle were filled, camps and cities of tents were constructed in the fields beyond the outer wall.

On the fifteenth day in May, in the year of 1692, the highly anticipated wedding of Miss Freyja Weir and Hugh Robertson MacCormac, took place in the early morning amidst hundreds of family and friends gathered in the Chieftain's Hall and adjoining corridors.

Despite her nervousness, Freyja looked beautiful in her dress, stunningly so in the mossy-green gown that Bethany had made for her. She held a bouquet of purple tulips, orange and yellow daffodils, bluebells, and purple anemones. Her bouquet mirrored the one Hugh had brought to the hunting lodge, down to the same lavender ribbon wrapped around the stem.

Bethany had covered Freyja's thick honey-blonde hair with a matching green silk kertch that she had made and brought with her especially for Freyja to wear.

The time had come, and Freyja couldn't believe she was actually getting married. She entered the Chieftain's Hall and spotted Hugh standing proudly in front of all who had gathered to witness their marriage. He cut a handsome figure of a man, dressed in his belted plaid, one portion draped over his shoulder and fastened with a silver bodkin. He wore a crisp white shirt and cravat, a dark blue coat, a sporran, stockings and a pair of new Ghillie brogues.

Hugh patted his right-hand pocket. Tucked into was a silver banded ring with a large emerald jewel set in the center. The ring once belonged to Hugh's mother, and he knew how pleased she would be to see it placed on Freyja's finger. Although, the lovely emerald could never match the brilliant sparkle of Freyja's eyes.

Freyja stepped into the hall and a sudden tightness spread across Hugh's chest. He drew in a sharp breath as she glided gracefully up the aisle toward him, a shy smile on her lips. Like the fool he was, he was overcome with lightheadedness, and as she stopped before him, he exhaled the breath he hadn't realized he was still holding. Her smile broadened across her lovely face. Leaning forward Hugh whispered in her ear, "Ye should be ashamed of yerself for what ye do to me, love."

"Aye, and ye to me," she purred back to him in a heavy Scottish accent."

Father Fitzgerald raised a thick white brow as he peered first at Hugh then Freyja. The wedding passed quickly and was followed by a hearty breakfast feast which was served in the large dining hall. The music stopped, signaling that it was time for Freyja's inauguration as chieftain and Laird of Clan Weir. Members of the Weir clan packed into the Chieftain's Hall once again, and several MacCormac and Sinclair clan members were also in attendance. Freyja taking the Oath of Fealty to the clan, was led by her cousin Duncan Lochlan Weir and the clan council. One single piper stood out on the cliffs, high above the sea and played a *piobaireachd*.

Still in her green dress, Freyja stood before everyone to swear her Oath of Fealty to her clan. "As my grandfather: Faolan Weir, my father: Lochlan Weir, and my brother: Andrew Weir, and all who ruled before me, I Freyja Weir of Clachan Craige do accept the responsibilities of Laird and Chief of Clan Weir. My commitments are to see that Clan Weir thrives and is well protected within my power." The white fox robe, symbolizing her leadership, was placed over her shoulders. Freyja almost flinched, then stood tall, honored to wear the chieftain's robe. She vowed to make her ancestors proud of her. A rumble filled the room as clan members chanted, "Laird Freyja Weir of Clachan Craige." A large chair, with a dragon carved into the back, was brought forward for Freyja to sit on and to rule from.

As her husband, Hugh, was the first to stand before his lady wife, Chieftain, and Laird, the hall grew quiet. On one knee before Freyja, his gaze met hers, and he said, "I swear me Oath of Loyalty and Fealty to my new laird. I promise to uphold the Weir Clan's customs, defend its people and holdings, and recognize, Laird Freyja Weir of Clachan Craige as my Chief." Freyja nodded her approval. Hugh stood, walked around her and took his place on her right. Clan members stepped forward, one-by-one to swear their Oath of Loyalty and Fealty to her. The ceremony took hours. By late afternoon, a large feast was presented in the dining hall, and Hugh and Freyja excused themselves to their chambers, ready to take on their new roles in the morning. Tonight was about the two of them being together, this time forever.

Later that evening, the celebration spilled out into the bailey, and Dreki Craige Castle came alive with music, laughter, and the spirits of drink and unity.

Cameron, Big Alec, and Malcolm strolled through the bailey, their stomachs full of rich food and sweets, their hearts filled with joy and contentment. "Weel, I'll confess," Big Alec said, taking another gulp of his ale. "I never saw this sort of situation coming."

"Aye." Cam shook his head. "Nor did I. I never would have believed Hugh would let such a strong-willed lass take him so far away from his kin."

Malcolm finished off his ale and laughed. "Weel, I tell ye, Hugh will never be able to control *that* wife."

Cam nudged Big Alec and nodded his head toward Malcolm. Grinning, Cam remarked, "'Twill soon be yer turn to be taking a wife of yer own, lad."

"Och, not me," Malcolm slurred. "*If*, I ever decide to marry," he held up his mug to emphasize his response. "She'll no be like yer wives. She will be a sweet and docile lassie. One who's kind and obedient." He looked up at the sky, starry-eyed, as if making a wish.

Cam exchanged a knowing look with Big Alec and they both laughed. Winking, Cam replied, "Good luck finding one of those, laddie."

THE END

THANK YOU FOR READING

~

Did you enjoy this book?

We invite you to leave a review at your favorite book site, such as Goodreads, Amazon, Barnes & Noble, etc.

DID YOU KNOW THAT LEAVING A REVIEW...

- Helps other readers find books they may enjoy.
- Gives you a chance to let your voice be heard.
- Gives authors recognition for their hard work.
- Doesn't have to be long. A sentence or two about why you liked the book will do.

About the Author

Whether I am writing a contemporary or an historical romance, my heroines will always be country girls, and my heroes will be alpha males. Two strong personalities locking horns, fighting to attain the ultimate prize in the end, makes for an exciting relationship.

I have been writing for years but have been dreaming up wild adventures my whole life. A time or two, I've even been lucky enough to have also lived a few.

Thank you for buying my books. I hope you enjoy them.

Lfnies1@yahoo.com
www.luannnies.com

Also by LuAnn Nies

WITH SATIN ROMANCE

MacCormac Warriors Trilogy

Faceless Angel

Fallen Angel

Novels

Shadow Trail

Catrina's Cowboy

Freeing Abigail

JoAnna's Rescue

Bearly Christmas Darling

Entitled

www.ingramcontent.com/pod-product-compliance
Lightning Source LLC
LaVergne TN
LVHW090605110826
845146LV00001B/272

* 9 7 9 8 8 8 6 5 3 4 5 0 4 *